To Suzu

THE *Time* WE *Met*,

doing a trip was
the best time ever!

by
Barbara Theesfeld

Barbara Theesfeld

Copyright © 2017 Barbara Theesfeld
All rights reserved
First Edition

PAGE PUBLISHING, INC.
New York, NY

First originally published by Page Publishing, Inc. 2017

This book is a work of fiction. Names, characters, and incidents are of the author's imagination or used fictitiously and are not to be thought of as real. Any resemblance to actual events, organizations, or persons living or dead (or ghosts) is entirely coincidental.

ISBN 978-1-64082-392-1 (Paperback)
ISBN 978-1-64082-393-8 (Digital)

Printed in the United States of America

To my two children, James and Genevieve; to my parents, Ray and Betty Mann who inspired me; and to Michael Reed who helped me find my smile.

To the memory of Wade Williams who was a gentle soul on this earth.

CHAPTER
1

Outside, the snow is gently falling, coating everything in a soft crystal fluffy blanket. Like the snow twirling in the wind as it lands on the ground and on my windowpane, so are my thoughts of days gone by. As it is the season of winter, so it is with me. But I am content. The year has reached the calendar end, and so has my life. But I am very content as the past eighty years have been full and rich. I couldn't have asked for a better life. It is days like these when the snow is falling and the sky is a melancholy gray, I like to sit and think back when I thought life and laughter would go on forever. And although my life is slowly coming to an end, I think of all the adventures I have had as a flight attendant dealing with all kinds of people and situations and as an artist. I think of the laughter we had in the back galley and on the van on our way to the hotel. I think of my children that I had borne and raised and the lovely times I had with my husband. The trips we went on and the sights we have seen were all wonderful. Even when the extensive traveling came to an end, and we both retired, our days were still full with sticky hands and wet kisses and gentle hugs from grandchildren.

However, there was once instance that I have never disclosed to anyone, not even my husband Alan, who would have thought me a bit touched in the head. I am not sure if it was a dream or if it was real, but it had a profound effect on me to the point that maybe it really could have been true. I am not sure. But I like to replay the memory of the strange encounter in my head, as it was really too sweet and too lovely to let go. I held on to the memory or the dream—or was it reality? It is not logical. And each time I think about it, there is a part of me that really does believe it truly happened.

As I close my eyes and lean my head back in my chair, I like to replay the scene over and over again.

I was a junior flight attendant for Equinox Air, and I remember that I had a two-hour delay, and I decided to get a bite to eat before my trip. I walked down the concourse to the food court which was always full of passengers and crew, who were taking a break and getting something to eat. I made my selection and balanced my food tray with one hand while pulling my suitcase, scoping out a place to sit down quickly before I spilled the contents of my tray. Every place was full except for just one empty table, and I weaved my way around the cluster of full chairs and tables and slid my tray down on the empty one I had spied. No sooner when I put my tray down, another tray came at the same time, and I looked up to see a gentleman who had the same idea as I.

"I think this is my table," he said.

"Excuse me, but I was here first," I replied, a bit annoyed at his gruffness. *Where are the chivalrous men these days, who would gallantly do anything for a lady?* I thought.

He looked around the food court and realized that there were no empty tables. He said to me sheepishly, "Since there are no other empty tables, can I at least sit down and share this one with you? I don't like to eat standing up actually."

I smiled at him and said, "Sure," and the moment of feeling territorial seemed to leave us both as we sat down and shook out our napkins.

"My name is Derrick. Derrick Graham," he introduced himself, holding out a very large and strong hand.

I took it and gently shook it, realizing how despite how strong it looked, it was a very soft and tender handshake.

"My name is Kit. Actually, Katherine Grey, but everyone calls me Kit."

We began eating our meal, and I could feel a sense of excitement surging up inside. *He is very handsome*, I thought to myself. He had salt-and-pepper hair and a neatly trimmed beard. The kind of beard that maybe a college professor would have. His eyes were warm and hazel in color. His eyes had a twinkle, and for whatever reason, he perked an interest in me, despite the fact the first impression was that he was being commanding and slightly rude.

"So where are you off to, Kit?" he asked in between bites of his burger.

"I have a Dallas turn. This is the last trip, and then I am done for two days and then off again for another four-day adventure," I replied.

He smiled. "That sounds like fun. I imagine you see a lot of different places."

"Yes and no. It just depends on how long the layover is and how tired I am. You would think that this is a glamorous job, but it really isn't. I mean, you have ten-hour working days, and you are on your feet constantly, and by the end of the day, you can't even feel them anymore. You have to deal with passengers who can be needy, demanding, and sometimes rude. But then on the other hand, it can be a lot of fun as you do meet some very nice people, and you do get time to explore where you are staying. I love it."

"How long have you been a flight attendant?" he asked me again. Derrick kept looking at me with interest. There was something about him that attracted me, but the reality of the situation was we were just two ships, or should it be airplanes, that pass in the night. He would finish his sandwich, and we would go our separate ways.

I replied, "I have been a flight attendant for two years now. I used to be a dietitian, but I got tired of it. Funny thing though, as a dietitian you are always telling people what to eat, and they never listen to you, and that is the reason why I got out of it. I am a flight attendant and no one listens to me! But at least the perks are better!"

We both laughed. I asked him, "So what do you do?"

"I am an engineer. I develop sensors with medical equipment. I am on my way to Montreal on business."

The banter continued on, back and forth, exchanging bits and pieces of ourselves, smiling and laughing and acting as if we knew each other forever. But we didn't. We were two strangers who were fighting over a table at a food court in an airport. *What were the odds of this?* I thought to myself as he was talking as to where this could possibly go. Did it matter where it went? I was attracted to him, and it seemed he was interested in me as we kept sitting there sharing stories and information. *What happens next?* I thought. *Do I suggest we exchange phone numbers? Is he married?* He didn't mention that bit of himself yet. As if he could read my mind, he said all of a sudden, "No, I am not married." He smiled at me, and his eyes looked hopeful that I would say the same to him.

"Neither am I," I said quietly.

I realized that time had really escaped me. Normally, I look at my watch while waiting on an airline delay, and thankfully, I had a half an hour to make my flight. What was supposed to be a five-minute lunch turned into an hour with only thirty minutes to spare.

"Look, I have to go to my gate. Derrick, it was really nice meeting you. I really enjoyed talking to you." I was trying to think what would happen next. *Fate, oh, please be kind, tell me what to do, or tell him what to do, but please don't let's just say goodbye.* I really hoped beyond hope that I would, could possibly get to know him more. As I stood up, he touched my arm. His eyes were hopeful, and his voice warm and kind.

"I know you have to go. So do I. I sat here longer than I should, but it has been delightful. I loved every minute of it, and I am thankful that the food court was full, and there was one empty table. I would love to talk to you more, and I would love to have dinner with you sometime. Could we do that?"

I said, "Yes, I would love that." I scribbled my name and number on a napkin, and he gave me his card. He lived outside of Saint Paul, not too far from where I lived, and again I thought, *What are the odds of that happening?*

"I get in tonight at nine thirty and am off for two days. But then I have a four-day starting Monday."

"I get up at ten, which would be your nine, but how about if I call you tomorrow, and we work out our schedules then? I don't get back to the States until next week, that Thursday. That is when you come in, right?" he said quizzically, trying to figure out the time logistics.

"Yes!"

"Then I will see you next weekend. I'll call, and we'll sort the going-out-to-dinner details then. OK?"

"Sounds good to me!" I said happily. *I must be crazy,* I thought as I just met someone at a food court and within an hour and a half made a date with someone I really hardly know. But deep inside I knew that this was not your usual fly-by-night as it were. I sensed something in Derrick right away. It was as if we clicked without any kind of effort.

I followed him, no, I floated along with him, as I was making my way to the gate. He smiled and said, "Are you going to Montreal with me instead?"

I then realized that I was going in the opposite direction of my gate. I laughed out loud. "And I *am* supposed to know what I am doing!" I said when I realized my mistake.

We both stopped in our tracks. He looked at me as if he knew me for years. I felt the same way. "I will call you tonight, Kit. Fly safe." He bravely and quickly kissed me on the cheek, which if anyone else had done, I would have been mortified, but this time, it felt comfortable as if we had known each other forever.

"Talk to you then," I said as I made an about-face toward my gate. I looked back to catch another glance, and at the same time, he did as well. He waved his hand toward me, and I did the same and then headed toward my gate. For a brief moment, I was in a happy fog, until I realized I had only twenty minutes to get to my gate in time where I picked up my pace, refocusing and getting my mind-set on the trip to finish.

CHAPTER
2

My Dallas turn seemed to go by quickly. I wasn't sure if it was because of the excitement of meeting Derrick or if it was just that I was in a good mood, or that the passengers were easy and agreeable. Maybe a combination of all three, but the time just flew by.

After we landed, I hurried back to my apartment. I waited by my phone like a school girl, and when it didn't after two hours of mentally willing the phone to ring, I gave up and went to bed thinking of how foolish I had been. But in the morning, I heard the tweet of a message coming in, and when I opened my phone, it was Derrick saying he was sorry he didn't call as he forgot there were international charges, and he wanted to keep the cost down. To me, that sounded reasonable. He assured me that he would call once he came back from "the dark side of the moon." I went on with my day, taking care of errands and thinking about him and really hoping he would indeed phone soon.

The days passed by with no new word, and I gave up the idea that he would even call me back. I felt foolish that I had let my fancies take over my mind and heart and decided that this was only just a moment in my life, and like all the other people and passengers in my life, they all just come and go. It was disappointing to me because from what I briefly knew about him, with just the scant information I had and the way he looked, I really liked him. I could still see his smile in my mind's eye. I could hear his voice and his laughter. I could easily remember his hazel eyes that seemed to look into my very soul. I would just have to get over it. I would just have to focus on the next set of trips on my schedule and get rested up and ready for that. Errands and laundry would keep me busy, as well as working out in the gym. I would just have to chalk it up as a brief encounter of the sweetest kind and leave it at that.

My four-day trip seemed long and laborious. The crew was pleasant enough, but I felt like the light that was lit in my heart had just been snuffed out. I just had to tell myself that it was a nice experience and to just let it go. Mine was a transient job. I met people going here and there, and it was ridiculous of me to think that anyone I would meet and talk with for an hour would be a lasting relationship. Things like that did not and would not happen to me.

After we landed and deplaned, I retrieved my suitcase from the designated crew bin. I turned on my phone, and there was a text message from Derrick.

I am sorry I didn't text you. I guess because international text messages have charges as well, but you were in my thoughts all week long. I knew you got in this afternoon and decided to wait for you in baggage claim. I don't know how long I am going to wait there, but it is worth it to make sure you understand I didn't forget about you.

I couldn't believe it. He had been waiting at baggage claim for me, not really knowing my flight or when I would be done. The silly boy had been waiting however long for me.

I charged out of the plane, saying a brief goodbye to my crew members, and they replied with grins "So where is the fire?" and "We weren't that bad, were we?" and then there was some mild laugher and curious looks as I was indeed in a hurry.

I walked as fast as my heels could take me down the concourse and then straight to baggage claim, sorting out the passengers from the main person I was looking for. I only saw him a week ago for just an hour, but he was so handsome that how could anyone forget, that I would not have trouble locating him in this crowd. And there he was, standing there with a bouquet of flowers that he got from one of the kiosks. It was like out of one of those cheesy romance movies. And here I was the lead actress.

He kissed me again on the cheek and then said a shy hi and handed me the flowers. "This is to make up for the fact I only texted you once. Canada is very expensive, and again, I was also really busy trying to work out specs and plans."

I took the flowers in hand and drank in the fragrance. I hadn't flowers given to me in such a long time. It was wonderful to be holding such a beautiful bouquet.

"Shall I take you home and drop you off, and then pick you up later for dinner? I know of a great Thai place in Saint Paul."

"That would be wonderful, but one thing I need to do first," I said to those smiling eyes of his.

"What's that?"

"I need to go back to the concourse and then come back so I can enjoy this all over again. What a wonderful way to arrive home after a tedious four-day trip."

"I can guarantee, my lady, that there will be more of this for you. I got a feeling on the first day that there was something special about you that I want to get to know more. I couldn't stop thinking of you all week long, and I couldn't wait to see you," Derrick confessed.

He looked at me tenderly and then took my hand. "Don't go back in, silly! Come out with me. I waited all week for you."

He picked up the handle of my suitcase, and we walked out together to the parking ramp, and again I felt as if I was in some sort of a dream: too flattering sweet to be real. But it was real, and he was taking me back to my place so he could pick me up later for dinner that night. For a brief moment, I thought this was about the most insane thing I could ever do—to allow a strange man that I have known for less than an hour take me back to my apartment. But I also knew in my heart that it would be OK, and the thought of my safety didn't cross my mind. I knew I would be safe in my heart.

Hours later, I found myself sitting across the table at one of the best Thai restaurants in town. Again, food was pecked at, and conversation dominated. Afterward we went to a cafe for dessert and coffee, not wanting the night to end but realizing it had to come to a close. He took me back to my apartment, and we still continued to talk in the car, again, neither one of us not wanting to leave.

"You know, one of us is going to have to be strong. Either I drive my car back to my place which I am not really ready for, or you are going to have to really say 'good night,'" he said quietly. I realized that it was getting late, and I had a lot to do the next day. I had laundry and repacking and going through mail and paying bills and running errands.

"Well, unfortunately, you are right. I have things that need to get done. I need to get to sleep … "

"And I will be dreaming of you," Derrick said softly.

At that moment, he took me in his arms and kissed me with all the tenderness and passion he could possibly evoke, and I felt all the energy leave me. I felt like there was nothing inside, and I was completely under his control, which I willingly gave to him. My mind went blank, and for a moment, I couldn't believe this was happening. How could I have met someone as wonderful and charming as this man, in a food court fighting for an empty table, and now we were locked in a kiss that melded us both into one? What if I decided not to have gone to the food court? What if I had decided to just get a snack at one of the magazine stores and gone directly to the gate which is what I normally would have done? Situations like this never happened to me, but it was happening now, and if I didn't leave now, things might be problematic, but in a delicious way of course.

Commanding my mind to work once again, I said, "I should go now." And with that, both car doors opened, and he walked me to the door. Derrick put his arms around me and kissed me again.

"When can I see you again, Kit?" he whispered into my ear. The warm breath of his sweet whisper fluttered against my ear and went through my body down to my knees, making them both weak.

"I really have things I need to get done tomorrow. And I leave the day after next for four days, so that leaves things for Thursday through Sunday when I get more time off."

"Then Thursday it will have to be, and hopefully the weekend."

We pulled apart, and I knew then if I didn't leave him now, he would be coming upstairs with me, and I didn't want to go that route at this point. Everything was too soon, but yet in a weird way, I felt like we had known each other for years.

He turned and walked down the sidewalk that led to my apartment but walked with a purpose, and as if he didn't, he would do an about-face and come up with me. He turned around and smiled at me, but then he made his way steadily back to the car.

I walked up the three flights of my apartment stairs and mechanically opened my door with my keys. I went to my chair and just reflected on the evening. I didn't want to move as I didn't want to break any spell that was hanging over me. And then I heard the tweet signaling a text.

> *To quote Shakespeare, "tis twenty years" till I see you again. How will I get through? So looking forward till then. Your Derrick.*

I wrote back:

> *I know. I didn't want the night to end. How did all this happen? A fight over an empty table? Really? The Fates have been looking out for us I am sure. Till then, I am as I ever was, yours. And in such a short time!*

Derrick texted back:

> *That will always be our table. If our traveling schedules match again, and we can meet for lunch like we did, that is our table, and we will just have to kick off whoever is there!*

To which I replied:

> *Yeah, and have TSA come over and give us grief for causing a ruckus!*

Derrick texted back:

> *And hopefully be put in solitary confinement with you!*

The texting went back and forth for another hour, as we couldn't seem to let each other go, but at one point, sleep was overcoming me, and I knew I had to get some rest. It had been a long day with a New York leg of trip, and then all the rest afterward. He finally sent me a text that said,

> *Good night, my dear sweet lady. I think I am falling in love with you … and so quickly … how could that be? What have you done to enchant my soul? Is it your bubbly personality? Is it your soft brown eyes and your gorgeous honey-color hair that hangs like silk down your shoulders? Is it your soft laughter or your sharp mind? I don't know, lady, but you have me lock, stock, and barrel!*

I didn't know what to say. It was too wonderful to be true, but I also had to understand that I had to be careful that I didn't get swept away by all of this only to have my heart crash and burn in the end. But then, I thought to myself, *Who cares?* He had me captivated by what I knew at this short time and the wonderful things he had just written. And something else inside of me just seemed to know that this was "the one."

> *Sweet dreams. And I am feeling the same way. Will miss you when I am gone, but I will come back to you. Good night, my dearest.*

My goodness! It was only a week ago that we just met, and we were falling fast and hard for each other. What was happening to us? I didn't understand any of it. I just knew two weeks ago I was by myself and resigned to be so. There was no one interesting in my life and didn't think it possible. It was hard to have a relationship with a flight attendant as we were always coming and going, but here, he wanted to be with me despite my crazy schedule. I couldn't believe how lucky I was, and with that thought, I put on my pajamas, crawled into bed, and turned off the light, but my mind could not shut off as I was thinking and dreaming of Derrick.

"Go to sleep!" I commanded myself. "Go to sleep, girl!" And as I willed myself to sleep, thoughts of Derrick and the possibilities of starting a wonderful relationship were blanketing me in sheer happiness.

CHAPTER

3

T he weeks passed to months, and the months melted into a year, and after a year of being with this wonderful man, he finally asked me to marry him. I didn't hesitate to say yes, and we planned to have the ceremony a year from when he asked me. It would give me time to get ready and plan the wedding and to get the time off from the airline.

I had met his mother and father who lived in Eagles Mere, which was a small town an hour north of the cities. They lived in a beautiful home, which overlooked a lake, and we had spent many a summer weekend when I had off with Douglas and Cynthia. Derrick and I went fishing at the lake or swimming with his family Gina, Carolynn, and his brother John. They had a crazy Labrador named Pilot of all names. The weekends were filled with picnics in the back-yard deck area, games in the evening, and long walks with Pilot. It was an idyllic summer that I would never forget.

I did notice that there were moments where Derrick would run out of energy doing the slightest activity but just reduced it to the fact that we were constantly going that summer. I would come home from my trips and either head to his place where we would take the drive up to Eagles Mere, or we would stay in the cities and go to the theater or dinner or just amble slowly away by the river, sitting by the riverbank, watching the planes fly overhead and think of how lucky we were to have found each other, at a table we had fought over. When I was on a layover or waiting for a flight to begin, I would go over to that table and sit there and replay in my mind that moment that we fought and met and then started to fall in love. I was grateful for that table and how it changed my life.

It was toward the end of the year, in December, six months before we were to get married, that I really began to notice Derrick dramatically slowing down. I was becoming worried about him and pushed him to go see the doctor. It was two weeks before Christmas when he was diagnosed with congestive heart failure, and he was going into a rapid decline. A week of hospitalization didn't seem to help, and we were at a loss as to how to help him. Derrick was far too young to be this sick, and even the doctors at Rochester didn't seem there could be anything to help him, other than a possible heart transplant if he got it in time.

Christmas Day was spent quietly. I drove him up to his parents, and we kept the celebration low-key. Normally the grandkids and cousins would be over, but it was cancelled so that there was less stress for Derrick until he could get a new heart.

I was afraid to go on four-day trips, so I signed up for day trips or overnight high-speeds so that I could be home either during the day or night. I felt the need to radically reduce my flying altogether so that I could be around to look after Derrick. His sister Gina helped out during the day, but at one point, it became too much for her, and it was then decided to get a nurse. With trying to juggle my schedule and worrying about Derrick, the strain was starting to wear on me. I wondered how long it would be until they could locate a heart for him before he would fade away.

There was a point when he started to improve. I wasn't sure if it was his sheer will to live and to hang on or all the prayers that were being sent up for him, but at one point, he started to gain a little more energy. I felt very hopeful. We still talked of getting married but were realistic that it wouldn't happen until he got his heart and he really improved.

His sense of humor had not diminished. He still was his witty self, saying silly things like trying to attempt to sing through his nasal cannula, "Don't Go Breaking My Heart" or that old Bing Crosby song "Be Careful, It's My Heart." He was trying to make light of the situation by finding any kind of heart-related songs. He was pale and puffing through each phrase, but his eyes were still shining like the day I met him. I didn't want to lose him. If I lost him, I wouldn't know what to do, but during those times, I could not let my mind go there. I had to hope and pray that a strong heart would come in time for him. It was morbid thinking that someone would have to die so he could live.

It was a warm day in April when the leaves were budding, and the air was fresh and clean. The winter slush of March mud was washed away by the early April rain and with the assistance of the city cleaners. I had finished a red-eye trip which despite the fact that it allowed me to spend my day with him, I was exhausted nevertheless from the lack of sleep.

"Can you get me a smoothie, darling?" he asked between breaths. His eyes, although shining, had dark circles. His face was paler than normal. He lifted his head off the lounge chair that he liked to sit in and reached over to give me a kiss. His arms were so thin. How did they get that thin? What did I miss? He kissed me but very gently as if it took all his strength just to do that, and any more would really wipe him out. I returned the kiss and then kissed him gently on his forehead. It seemed cold to the touch. I pulled his blanket up closer to warm him.

"I'll be back soon, Derrick love," I said.

"Get me raspberry," he puffed back.

"You got it."

"And I love you," he said. I turned back to look at him as I was getting my purse, and he said, "I will never forget fighting over that table. It was the best fight I ever had with anyone. And I won. I won you, and not the table."

"I know," I said. "That was the best day of my life. You are the only one who makes me float. You know that. You are the only man that could ever make me float. Really, really." My eyes were starting to well up with tears. "I love you so much."

I stopped to look at him. He looked so small in the chair, despite the fact he was a tall man. He was sinking into the chair as if it was going to engulf him. In a nanosecond, I thought back to the lovely days of being on the lake, of laughing, of loving, and here he was looking so small and weak with being connected to an nasal cannula. This was not the picture I imagined, but yet, I would not have left him to deal with this on his own. I loved him that much. I wanted that time back. I didn't know if that was a possibility, but I wanted the old healthy Derrick back. I wanted things the way they used to be. They could still be, if there was a heart, but each day looked less likely possible that there would be enough time left for him. The real truth was he was dying.

He smiled at me weakly and then said in a near whisper, "I love you so much."

When I came back with the smoothie, he was gone. My Derrick, my love of my life was gone.

I stared at him for a moment, thinking it wasn't possible. Time just froze. I froze. When did it get so cold in that apartment? A million thoughts collided in my brain and froze them in a moment. He was just faking me out. He was playing games with me again. He was just sleeping. No. He was … gone. He was gone. It kept going over and over in my head. He was gone. I touched his still body. The Derrick that I knew and loved was gone. And he wasn't coming back. He was gone. What happened in the meantime? I just talked to him less then fifteen minutes ago. But no, he was gone. I looked at him in disbelief. And then I had to call 911. I had to make the call. While I waited for the ambulance to come, the apartment seemed surreal. It was quiet. Everything around the apartment looked strange and cold. I felt like everything had been sucked out of me, and I was alone. I was all alone. The laughter, the tears, the loving, the Saturday nights, the Sunday mornings, the days in the warm sun cuddling by the river at our rock, the endless trips to the doctor, and the hospital … it was all over. Derrick was gone. It was over.

CHAPTER
4

It was surreal. Time stopped. But at the same time, it went forward. People moved fast, and then at the same time, they moved as if in a dream. I called 911 after trying to do CPR myself. It was useless. He was gone. The color drained from his face. I could feel the warm leave his body. It was melting out of him, and unfeeling coldness took its place. I looked for anything that resembled life. There was nothing. He was gone. The EMT's called and then looked at me apologetically and said he was gone. The final words, he was gone. I was ushered into another room, and I could hear them unhooking him from his oxygen. I could hear them shift the body, his body to a stretcher, and as I peeked out from the corner, I could see them wheel him out. I don't know what happened next. I wasn't sure what to do. I looked at the chair where he was and it was empty. The useless equipment was left behind. So was the table stand that had his medications and his glass. The slippers were without an owner, the robe that he wore was draped causally over the chair, and his lap blanket was in a pile on the floor.

I went over to the robe and breathed in its scent and drank in the smell of what was Derrick that would never be again. I closed my eyes and then I wept because he was really gone. The man that I fell in love with, the man that I thought was my soul mate, the man that I thought I would spend the rest of my life with was gone and would not come back no matter how much I cried and pleaded and begged God for it to be some kind of cosmic joke and he would be coming around the corner, laughing and saying, "I am just kidding you Kit. I am fine!"

I fell in a pile at the foot of his chair and just didn't know what to do. I heard a voice enter the room and it was someone from EMT. "Are you going to be ok? " He quietly asked. "Is there anyone around to help you, can I call someone for you?"

I looked up at him and he looked at me with such kindness and empathy. That show of kindness made me want to cry. He knew that this was not easy for me and had the sincerity to come back and check on me. I looked up at him and told him that I would be ok (not) and that I would call my sister who lived not too far and I would probably stay with her.

"Can I stay with you until someone comes?" He asked as he got done on one knee and took my hand.

"No, I will be ok (not). I just want to be alone. (I think)."

"If there is anything I can do, give me a call. It is not generally done with our group but I totally understand as I lost my wife two years ago and it is not easy." He wrote down his number and I took it and put it in my pocket. His name was Pat Mahoney. He actually lived in the complex next to where Derrick lived and where I was going to be. "I am next to you. I live in the River Walk apartments. If you need help with anything please let me know.

He really did seem sincere and wanting to help. Did I look that vunerable? I probably did. I felt so alone. Like I was in another sphere, like in a dream or a bubble where I couldn't feel but yet at the same time every nerve was spiking in my body.

"Thank you. I will be ok, I just got to make a few calls."

"Can I help? Can I do that for you?" he asked.

"I will be ok. I just need to ....call. I need to call his parents, his family and my in flight supervisor, I need to call my sister....I need to call ...

And then I broke down. I don't know what happened next but this kind gentleman, took over for me. He made the calls while I gave him the number. I couldn't do the calling except to my in flight and they were kind enough to give me as much time as I needed to have.

When that was done, I needed to call my sister Suzanne. She promised to come over straight way. As I was waiting for her, I walked around the apartment thinking how empty this place was now that he was gone. He wasn't just gone to the grocery store or to work or in the laundry room washing his shirts for the week. He was gone. I believed in a heaven, and a God, and I believed that was where he was, but was he lurking around watching me fall apart?

And how could a home like the one we were going to have, be so empty? Everything looked so lonely. Nothing seemed to belong to anything or anyone anymore. Some of my things had been slowly moved over, in preparation for me to be eventually be living here, but what was here seemed out of place. They were correct (and who was they) that said 'You can't take it with you.' What did all of these things mean? They were nothing now. But at the same time they were everything. They were everything that was his.

As I was waiting for Suzanne, all at once I thought I couldn't breathe. I had to get out of here before the tusami of saddness flooded me and made me emotionally frozen. I did. I charged out of the apartment and ran down the steps instead of waiting for the elevator to get me out of this place. I couldn't stay another minute.

I sat outside on a park bench. Ironically one that was placed right across the street from his deck. I could see that the lights were off and it was dark inside. It would be forever dark inside. And even if there was a light it would not be his light. I wrapped my sweater around me despite the fact that the sun was shining and the breeze was warm and gentle. The birds were singing. People were walking up and down the sidewalk enjoying the morning stroll with their dogs or with each other. They had no idea that my heart was breaking and crumbling into bits. They had no idea that my life was over. "Why was it so sunny", I raged inside my head. Why is this such a nice sunny warm spring day? Why are the birds singing? There is no reason for birds to be singing on this dark dismal day. Oh how I wanted to shout out at the birds and at the smiling faces that no one had any right to be happy on this lamentable day. What was I going to do now that he was gone? How could I carry on? How could I possibly enjoy another day with out him. I felt as if I was faced with some kind of emotional dead end. How was I going to get through this without crumbling into a million pieces. I wanted to find a dark hole and crawl into it because I knew I would never be able to face the days ahead. When I thought I could not even tolerate one more minute being outside, or being just anywhere, I saw Suzanne's car pull up and as she rolled down the window she ordered me to get in.

Before she took me to her home, she took me out for coffee. That was about all I could handle at this point. It was even hard to drink the coffee but I drank it anyway.

"Were are your clothes? Are they at Derricks or at your place?" she asked me.

"I have a suitcase at his place."

"Ok. When we are done here, I'll go up and get your case and your cosmetics. You are staying with me for a couple of nights. I don't want you alone and I don't want you at Derricks."

I nodded in agreement. I didn't think I could go back up there, at least not now. Actually I didn't want to be anywhere at the moment. I just wanted to be vaporized away.

Suzanne took my hand and then said gently, "Kit. He was sick for awhile and you know that he really wasn't getting any better."

I sniffed back in agreement again. "I just thought that he would hang on till he could get another heart. I should have done a better job at looking after him. I should have taken a leave of absence. I don't know, I just can't believe that in a nanosecond he is gone. All I did was go out and get him a smoothie. I just left for a few minutes." The tears began again.

"He probably picked that time and that moment for him to slip away. He probably didn't want you to see him take his leave. You shouldn't beat yourself up for that Kit. He loved you so much, and maybe that was his kind way of leaving. Having you watch him take his last breath would have been perhaps far more difficult for you. "

I didn't say anything. I just felt numb from it all.

"Just remember he loved you so much. When he looked at you when you weren't aware, he just glowed. I kind of envied you. I wish I had that."

Again, I didn't say anything, I just felt numb from it all.

Suzanne was finding it to be a loss to comfort her sister. "And I do believe that you will find someone else to love you in the same way as Derrick did. You are a beautiful women and too lovely a person to be hid in a closet."

At that moment, I could feel a small rage well in at me. "No. I won't find anyone else that will love me in the same way Derrick did. Derrick was my soul mate. We felt and thought the same way. We were cut from the same cloth bolt. We were dry clean only. No I won't find anyone else that I will love or will love me ever again. I want my Derrick back with me." And then I broke down in a cascade of tears. I could feel people discretely staring at me wondering what was wrong and I didn't feel the least embarrassed. I wanted everyone to know and understand my pain. I wanted everyone to know that this was a horrible day and I didn't care in the least bit at how selfish a thought that was. I wanted to kick and scream and rage and at the same time I wanted to crumple down and have someone hold me and never let me go.

"I am so sorry I said that Sis. I didn't mean it that way. Come on. Lets go…let me get you home and tuck you in. You need a glass of wine and a good nap. Let me take care of you."

Another flux of emotions over came me again, and I felt limp as Suzanne help my arm as we walked out the coffee shop. I wanted to get my things, and I wanted to go and lay down. Somewhere where it was dark. And somewhere where I could sleep and hopefully never wake up.

CHAPTER
5

The next few days passed in a numbing blur. The ache in my heart was at times overwhelming, but I knew I had to make it through to the funeral without breaking down. I knew Derrick would want me to be strong. I could feel it. When I wanted to break down in an emotional mess, I could almost feel him holding me on. When I wanted to break down and cry, I could feel a puff of strength, and I could make it to the next order of business.

The funeral was held in Eagles Mere. It was a simple and beautiful ceremony. He would have liked it; I am very sure of that. The hard part was not necessarily the memorial service or the burial, but afterward when it was over. The funeral lunch was held at the family home, and for me, that was the hard part.

There was the usual spread of donated food and casserole dishes. But I had no interest in eating, although Carolynn was there, hovering with a plate of food, trying to encourage me to eat. I just wanted to be alone. I left the crowded dining and living room of guests and relatives to go for a walk down by the lake. Each step reminded me of the many picnics and parties and boating afternoons that we spent together before he became ill. It was painful but yet comforting at the same time to think of these moments and remember them. I could almost see him on the lawn playing horseshoe during family gatherings. I could remember walking together in the evening toward the lake, after a lovely dinner that Cynthia prepared. The air would be slightly cool from the breeze from the lake, and air would be sweet and gentle. We would walk toward the bench and then just sit and watch the moon shine on the water and just talk about our future or gently nuzzle each other until we were in a full-blown kiss. It was always so magical, and I never wanted it to end. But it did.

I sat there on the bench that we used to share, and I felt so lonely. It was too much to bear, but at the same time, I wanted to be here. I wanted to remember everything all at once, and I wanted to make sure it would be on the hard drive of my brain forever. I didn't want to lose any of this. But at the same time, I felt like I was going to lose this, and things would never be the same again.

Emotion was starting to well up in me, and then all of a sudden, I felt a flutter against my shoulder. I looked over, and it was nothing. But it felt warm and gentle, and it had a smell that was ever so sweet but at the same time tinged almost earthy-like. I felt curious, but then there was nothing there. I attributed it to just a casual breeze coming off the lake. But in a strange way, it comforted me. I didn't feel like I was going to break down again. I felt at peace. I closed my eyes and again tried to remember the good times we had. I didn't ever want to forget them.

"Hey you, Kit!" I turned around, and it was John. It was some-how painful yet comforting to look at John as he looked very much like his brother Derrick. He had that strong handsome face and hazel eyes that Derrick had. "What are you doing here by yourself? Are you OK?" John came over and slid aside of me on the bench. "I am a little worried about you, Kit." He took his arm and put it around my shoulder. I welcomed it. It felt good.

"I am doing OK. Sort of," I replied.

"Hey, Kit, I know it is going to be tough, but we are all here for you. Mom and Pop and the rest of us. We knew how much Derrick loved you, and you are still a part of the family. That is not going to change one bit."

"Thanks. I was kind of worried because, well, you know how it is sometimes."

"I do, I do," John said thoughtfully. "But not with us. You will be welcome to any family event, and of course, I would love to keep in touch with you ... like say coffee or something."

"That's nice. I appreciate it. I love this family, and I was really afraid I would lose you all."

"Never! Never!" John said emphatically. "You will always be a part of the family no matter how your life goes. We all adopted you. You took such good care of Derrick toward the end. You did all you could, and we all appreciate it."

"I don't feel like I did," I said, feeling the tears start up again.

"Yes, you did. You took marvelous care of him, and you couldn't have done it any better. Just know that. You gave everything you had to make sure he was comfortable. You did all you could, and you should never question that. You have given him the last two years of his life, the very best. He was so happy with you. I used to get calls from him, and his voice was so light and cheerful and excited when he would talk about you. You made him very happy."

I felt good and at the same time very sad. What a conflict of emotion that goes on with grief. Up and down and around and around, happy, sad, mad, frustrated, content, and then resigned. Why one couldn't just go through these emotions methodically and one at a time and then discard them, when one is done? It just seemed like an endless merry-go-round of feelings, and I just wanted to get off.

We sat there quietly for a little while, and then John said, "It's time to get moving, Kit. I can drive you home if you like." I thanked him. I could see that back at the house, the crowd was thinning out, and people were getting ready to go home, or they had already done so.

As we walked back to the house and the family, he linked his arm with mine. It gave me strength somehow to face the family again without having to well up again for what seemed like the billionth time.

"Tomorrow we are going to go to the apartment and finish cleaning it up," John said. "I know you still have some stuff at his apartment, and there are probably some keepsakes you would like to have. The family will be there about nine o'clock. I know this will be again painful for you, but again, you are welcome to come over and help, or you can tell us what you would like and where your stuff is, and we'll take care of it for you."

"No, I would like to come over. I can do this," I replied. "It has to be done."

"Do you want me to come and get you?" John asked.

"No, that is OK. I can drive."

It was settled, and tomorrow, I would have to face another phase of all of this, which would be the cleaning up, the closing up, and the final ending. The cousins had already begun the process, but there was still more to do.

Douglas and Cynthia were saying goodbye to the final wave of people leaving to go home. *They are both holding up very well,* I thought to myself.

"Kit. I just want to tell you that you will always be a part of this family. Don't ever forget that. I will always consider you my daughter-in-law no matter what. Derrick just loved you to pieces, and I have never seen him happier than when he was with you."

Tears started to trickle down my face again. It was overwhelming, the love that his family had for me despite the fact I was never an official Graham. I hugged them both, and then Carolynn held my hand and said, "You are welcome here anytime. You can come here for lunch or coffee anytime you want. We will always be here for you."

"Thank you," I said. "I love you both so much. I don't know what I would do if I would lose you too."

"You won't lose us," Douglas said. "You are stuck with us, I am afraid!" he said with a grin.

"I couldn't imagine anyone else I would want to be stuck with."

Then with another round of hugs and kisses, John took me home. This time, this time I would have to be with myself and myself alone. As I lay in my bed that night and stared out the window, I realized that there would be no final calls from Derrick; there would be no texting. There would be no "good night, sweetheart" or any of that. There would be no good-night kisses or hugs or evening cups of tea. It was just quiet, and this is what I would have to cope with. Thankfully, I had my daughter, and although she was hurting just as much as I, she would be a real comfort to me.

The next day, I arrived at the apartment. Family members were there in the final process of boxing and cleaning and sorting. They must have arrived earlier as I was on time. There was just a flurry of activity and work, and in some ways, it was disturbing to me. The hospital equipment was put away and boxed and marked. The sheets that lined his chair and the blankets were in a heap ready for the wash. The table next to the chair was put away. I walked around the apartment that we shared, and there were people in every room working as busy as beavers cleaning and sorting and putting away and throwing out. I felt violated again. This was where he lived. This is where I stayed on the weekends, this was where I had my things, this was where we ate dinner and watched TV and lived and loved. Everything was being dismantled, and I felt like I was being dismantled. A cousin, who I remembered her name as being Claire, was in the bedroom pulling out more clothes from the closet. Thankfully, I had retrieved some of his shirts for my own personal keepsakes.

"I am just cleaning out the closet for clothes to donate," she said sheepishly. "That is what John told me to do."

I grabbed another shirt and breathed in the scent, trying to find Derrick again. "I want these," I said. And I wondered why as I already had three of his shirts. What would I do with them except smell them, trying to bring him back to me in that way, and remembering the times we had when he wore those shirts. Why did I need more? I needed more because I know I would never have enough. But I also had to be sensible.

"Well, OK," Claire said. And she stood back as I scoped out his closet. My mind went back to when we were going to get ready to go out to dinner or to the theater or some event. He would be pausing over the selection of shirts looking for the right one. I grabbed a few more shirts I remembered him wearing for special occasions. I wanted to keep these. I found an empty box and then started piling some of his things, as well what I had there. It wasn't much, but it was enough to establish the fact that I was a part of this place, a place that was being dismantled of Derrick forever.

Each room of the apartment reminded me of an event or a time. I would go back for a brief moment in time and reflect as to what we were doing or what the activity was. I wandered back out into the living room, and it was becoming too much. I had to get the rest of my stuff and leave. But then again, I was glad that the family was tackling this job as I just couldn't do it myself.

I collected my things and things I bought him over the course of time, and then some keepsakes and put them in a box and then thanked John who was busy going over Derrick's bills and letters and other important paperwork that needed to be attended to. He walked me to the door, and I apologized for not doing more, but he understood. The situation of all of this was sad. Just last week, Derrick was alive, sitting in the chair, watching something on TV while I was making him some soup for dinner. How things radically change in just a short period. But I had to leave as it was becoming too much for me. I had to get out.

I was able to drive but was thankful when I got home. But it was far too quiet. There was nothing I wanted to do, but to break down in a million pieces and never be put back together again. I remembered there was a bottle of vodka I bought at one time that I barely touched. I think I had bought it for New Year's or something, but I remembered it was there. I got the bottle, and it was full. *Good,* I thought to myself. I am going to drink this whole thing and maybe never wake up again. I can't bear this quiet. I can't bear this day. I can't bear being without Derrick. I can't stand the pain that is far too much for me to bear. I can't bear not being without Derrick anymore. I was just going to drink this to an oblivion. And hopefully never wake up.

I got myself all comfortable on the couch and decided to forgo the glass and just chug this right out of the bottle. I closed my eyes and took a swig. I took a large swig. The liquid burned down my throat, but I didn't care. The vodka began its business. I could feel my nerves being numb and the sadness being melted away. If I could make it through the entire contents of the bottle, then it would be all over. I could be with Derrick in another world, forever. No more loneliness again. No more pain, no more sadness. I tilted the bottle for another long major drink, and then all of a sudden, I heard a voice say to me in a strong and authoritative and familiar tone, "Put the bottle down now. Put the bottle down now, and get your hands off the bottle and step away from it now!"

I put the bottle down, mostly in fear, and then looked up. There it was. No, there he was. It was Derrick. It was Derrick in the flesh? Or was it the spirit? I wasn't sure as I was feeling a little drunk by this point, but it, whatever it was, looked like Derrick, and he was all healthy and pink and ruddy looking as he did when I met him. But whoever it was, Derrick or a hallucination from being drunk, was very angry at me, and for a moment, I was a little scared.

CHAPTER

6

I wasn't sure if it was the amount of alcohol I had just consumed, or my grief pushing things larger than life, or if the vision was totally real, but there was Derrick standing in my living room, looking better than I had ever seen him. He was youthful but yet mature. He looked healthy. He never looked better, and for a moment, I was really confused. Had we not gone through a funeral for him? Who was in that coffin then? Or was this the alcohol and my grief just manifesting itself in this vision that was too fanciful to be true? I wanted it to be true, but I felt hesitant to react so I just sat there gobsmacked.

"Kit! What are you doing? Stop that now. Put the bottle down and stop this!"

"I ... I ... OK ... " I stammered. "Derrick, is that ... really ... you? Didn't we just bury you a few days ago?" I still wasn't sure what to make of this. Do I run over and hug him now that he is back? I wasn't sure how to react. Is this a Lazarus moment that I am experiencing? I just didn't know what to do.

Derrick moved closer and then sat down on the lounge chair, but as I looked closely, I could still see the lounge chair cushion. He was indeed a ghost or just a hallucination of the vodka that I had just consumed. I could feel the adrenaline move through my system, immediately sobering me up.

"It really is me. I am no illusion, but I have been given some leave from up there to stop you from chasing after me. You are not ready to go where I am, until you are ready to do so. Don't hurry things along when you are not supposed to. And besides, Lizzy still needs you."

"Derrick," and then I began to cry, "I miss you so much. I can't tell you how hard life is without you now. I never expected to lose you. I thought you would hold on till we got a new heart for you, and I did everything I could to help you, but I feel like I failed somehow. I just want to be with you, wherever you are."

I grabbed what was left of the tissues. I had gone through so many. I was so tired of crying.

"I know, my love, I know," he said softly. "I miss you too, and I saw that you were hurting so badly from up there. But you can't follow me. Not just yet. You have a wonderful life ahead of you. You have so many chapters in your story to write. You are not done yet with your life here on earth. As much as we loved one another, I was just a part of your story. I wasn't the completion. You gave me the best time of my own life, and I will always cherish that time we had together. But you, my dear, need to go on with your life. Think of the good times we had and hold that fast. Treasure it but move on with your life and love again."

"I can't. I can't begin to think of loving anyone but you ever again. You were my soul mate. You and I were one. Remember what we used to say? We used to say we were cut from the same cloth. 'Dry clean' only."

"We were at the time, but there will be others that will come in your life that will be your soul mate. I refuse to believe that we were given only one. Maybe some people were, and they lived long and happy lives. But as my life was cut short, for whatever reason, there will be other people that will finish your sentences, like the same things you do, laugh at the same kind of movies, and love like the way we did. You need to move on. Grieve for me if you must, but don't grieve in sorrow of what might have been, but think of me as all the good times we did have. Think on those things. Think of the weekend trips we took to go to the cabin up north and looked for moose and went fishing. Remember going up to Mom and Pops and the weekend picnics, the games on the lawn, the lunches on the patio or the boat. Think of the luscious times we had together by the fire. Remember that and smile. Don't weep for me. It won't be too long before it will be your time, after a full life, after loving more, and I will be waiting for you. But your time is not now."

Then he was gone. I wanted to talk to him more. I had more to say to him, but he just vanished as quickly as he appeared. I looked down at my bottle and thought that he was right. It was a silly and stupid idea. I put the bottle away and then decided to try to take on the day, not too sure how, but if that is what he wanted me to do, then I must. How I was going to navigate through these empty days that lay ahead, I wasn't sure, but I would try. I had to, at least, for him. If this was a mirage from being drunk, or a reality, I was going to take advice from that and move forward. I had a warm feeling that Derrick would want me to do that. I could again feel the warmth around my body and soul that not only did he want me to do that, but I would have to do that. If anything, I needed to be there for Lizzy. She would need me, and I was wrong to think that I had a right, in the depths of my despair, to follow Derrick into the larger life.

The next few days were still hard. I had a hard time trying to fall asleep, and I had a hard time just being in the apartment. I felt a huge desire to be with people, but then when I was with people, like in a park or the corner coffee shop, I felt like I wanted to be at home. I was restless and couldn't settle. I couldn't focus in one place. I needed to be distracted somehow. What better place to do it than work.

I went back to work after being off two weeks, and it felt good to walk down the concourse. I felt energized. I felt that this is what Derrick would want me to do. But there were places I couldn't go to. I couldn't go to the food court. I had gone there, and I got myself an egg sandwich that morning and was about to find a place to sit, when I saw the table where we met. I could almost see us sitting there in my mind's eye when we first met. I had to leave. I had to find another place to eat. I decided to go to the crew room.

There were some of my friends in the crew room, killing time, waiting to go to their perspective gate. As soon as I came through the door, I was greeted by my friends. I received hugs, condolences, and more hugs and sad looks. It triggered me again into floods of tears when I was doing so well. I was almost sorry I came there to eat my breakfast sandwich.

At that moment, my best friend Diane came into the crew room. She nearly dropped her bags when she saw me standing there. She rushed over and gave me the biggest hug ever. It felt good, as I felt a surge of strength coming from her body into mine.

"Hey, gurl! How ya doin'?" she said to me.

"I am hanging in there," I said quietly. I wiped away my tears because Diane was not one for a lot of sentiment. She would have her pity party, but for five minutes, and then she expected others to move on with theirs as well, including me.

"Well, you got to, gurl," she said in a firm tone. Her dark eyes looked at me fiercely. That was what I loved about her. She was sympathetic but not one for a lot of mushy sentiment and heartfelt slop. She charged ahead with her life with a gusto that always inspired me. "You got to, gurl," she repeated. "Derrick would want you to do that. He wouldn't want you to set around and feel sorry for yourself. You had a good run with him, and for that, you should be very grateful. You got your job here that you love, you have friends here that you love. Don't lose that by getting too engulfed in grief that don't serve no purpose. Yeah, grieve for him but not in a sorry way. Be glad for the times you got with him."

I realized it was exactly what Derrick had told me. It was true. There wasn't really anything to feel or be sorry for. I had a wonderful time with him, and he was sick. That was just it in a nutshell.

"You gotta trip?" she said as we sat down in one of the chairs. "Where you going?"

"I have an overnight to San Francisco. I get there at ten and then come back tomorrow afternoon. Not too bad for the first trip back. I have two days off and then have a three-day after that."

"Sounds good. Work will be good for you. It will get you back on track faster," she said with some affirmation. "Hey! I gotta get going! I gotta check in and then get up to my gate! I forgot the time, but I am so glad to see you, Kit!" She hugged me again, and I knew then I was going to be all right. At least for today.

"If you need to talk, don't hesitate to call me, but each day will get better and better. I promise," she said as she made her way to take her leave.

"I know," I said. After she left, I felt able to carry on. I felt a little stronger. Until another flight attendant came in and saw me and ran over to give me another warm hug. The hugs were nice. The kindness and love that was flowing through the crew room and through the flight attendants and pilots were wonderful until someone said, "I am sorry, but just know he is in a better place." Then I lost it all over again.

CHAPTER
7

I had grown to hate to hear the phrase "He is in a better place." What better place could it be than with me? But I also became to understand that people didn't know what to say other than "He is in a better place." What can you say? "I'm sorry" seems so simple. But then they are sorry. They are sorry that the deceased is gone. And they are truly sorry for the ones who are grieving. There doesn't seem to be any phrase in the English language or any other language for that matter, which anyone can say that will make one feel better. People struggle to find the right words, but somehow the pain of the loss is always there.

That is how I felt. As I walked up to my gate, I felt that I was moving forward with my life in returning to work, but I felt empty. There was no one to say goodbye to, no one to talk to. My routine before leaving was altered, and I wasn't sure how to deal with it. It felt strange to me. But it quickly evaporated when I met my crew members, and they didn't elaborate on a lot of sympathy, which was good. I didn't need to have heartstrings plucked. I wanted to get on with my day.

And I did. My trip went smoothly as it always had gone before. The day passed quickly, and so did the flights, and before I knew it, I was in my hotel room, and then the feelings of sadness and anguish started to rear its ugly head. My routine would be calling Derrick as to how my day went. I would jump out of my uniform and put on lounge clothes or pajamas, and when comfortable, I would give him a call. Now, the routine was altered, and there was no one to call. There would be no text messages of "good nights" and "I miss you." The room seemed horribly quiet, so I turned on the television to create some noise and diversion, and it worked for a while, but when I turned off the TV and settled into bed, the phone sat quiet on my nightstand. It would not ring or send me a text. And that is when the tears started all over again.

Work was a great diversion until I came home. I was happy to be done with my four-day but at the same time scared. I lumbered off the jet bridge with my crew, into the noisy gate area, and it was a little overwhelming with people everywhere along with the noise. I was eager to get out of the concourse area, but at the same time realized that there was no one to pick me up at passenger pickup. If Derrick was home, he would be there waiting for me to come out of the airport and take me home. But it was not going to happen this time. I made my way toward the light rail as this was going to have to be my mode of transportation now.

I was at the point at the airport where if I turned right, I would be at the passenger pickup. To my left was the escalator to the light rail. I froze for a moment. My feet wishing to go to the passenger pickup but my head knowing that part of my life was over. I stared out the window, watched all the cars pull up and the people greeting their friends or lovers or husbands/wives and then hoisting their suitcases in the trunk. I closed my eyes for a moment and thought back to that time when it was me waiting for my Derrick. I thought back to the first time he picked me up and how special it felt to see him there waiting for me. But it was not to be anymore. There was no one to go home to. And for a moment, there was no place to go to and nowhere to be. I wanted to turn around and go back to the concourse and either fly away or go to the crew room and see if I couldn't pick up a trip. Go anywhere but home.

I arrived at the apartment and realized I had four days off. Four days to fill my time with. Four days to figure out what to do. Four days to be by myself. What would I do? My friends were flight attendants, and they were all on a trip or getting ready to go on one.

I peeled off my uniform and threw it in a pile on the floor. I
didn't care. I got into some jeans and a T-shirt and pulled my hair
back into a ponytail. I just slumped down on a chair and wondered
what next. I had to do something. I was always happy to go home.
Most of the time I went straight to Derrick's, no, our apartment, and
we would happily plan out the next three days. If he wasn't home, I
would take a nap until he arrived, and then we would either go out to
dinner, or he would make a light meal and then spend the rest of the
evening cozy on the couch watching TV and just being happy being
together. I shut my eyes.

"We have theater to go to tomorrow, don't we?" I said happily.

"That's right! And I thought we would go out for dinner before
the show," he said as he kissed me. "And then maybe a quiet cocktail
afterward. How would you like that?"

"Sounds wonderful! Anything to be with you…"

Was it just last year when all of this started? And now what?
Nothing. No theater, no dinners, no movies, no nothing to look forward to. A great black hole of nothing.

I had to get out of that apartment. Maybe go up and get a
coffee. Should I go to the park and take a book? Should I go for a
walk along the river? I got a light jacket and got ready to go out. But
where to go? I felt like I had no direction, no compass, no plan or
list of what to do. It was overwhelming. It was then I burst into tears
thinking I should have finished off that bottle of liquor. Oblivion
was better than being here.

"What is going on here?" a familiar voice said.

"Huh?" I sniffed. I wiped my eyes with a tissue and then did a
double take. It was Derrick. He was back. I was so happy to see him
again, but at the same time, I was a bit startled and not sure if I could
believe my eyes. This time I wasn't drunk. I was actually very sober.
Very depressed but sober.

"I heard you crying from the other side and had to see what
is going on now. I thought you had a good trip with your crew and
passengers? What happened?"

"I did," I sniffed again. "I actually did. But the going home was kind of tough because there was 'no you' to come home to. There was 'no you' to call or text in the evening."

"Well, it is a little hard to text or phone where I am at, but I am allowed a glimpse of what is going on with you for now, and it pains me to see you in this state, Kit."

Derrick moved closer to me, only this time he didn't sit down. "Kit, you need to pull yourself together. It's not so bad. We had each other for that brief but joyful time, and you should think on those happy memories and be grateful for just that. You need to move on though."

"How can I? How can I move on without you?"

"You can, and you will. You are young enough and beautiful enough that you will move on. You won't forget about me, but you will tuck those memories of us in some special compartment in your heart, and at the same time, make new memories and happy times. I guarantee that."

"I just don't know how," I said through another flood of tears. "It hurts too much."

"Then feel the hurt. But just for a little bit. And at the same time you are feeling the hurt, do something."

"Like what?" I said, not really understanding any word he was saying.

"Anything. Read a book, go for a walk, which is what I thought you were going to do. Make a meal, a dessert, snacks. Get some canvas and paint, blog something, just do something, Kit. Don't sit here and weep for me. I am fine! I miss you from where I am at, but I have to move on too. I am given only a little time to help you understand that what we had was wonderful, but it wasn't the 'end' as it were, but only a part of who you are and where you are going. I was only in your life for just a season. Better days are ahead."

"But better days was when I was with you," I quietly said.

"Those were good days, weren't they?" he said as he smiled at me. Oh, how I missed that smile. I missed that look in his eyes that were bright and loving. I missed feeling him and being held by him.

"Oh, they were, and I could have gone on forever with you. I could have."

"I know, I too. But the Fates had it different for me, and for you and whatever you are directed, whatever direction you go, whatever turbulence or smooth air you experience, I will always be with you, in your heart. You will never lose that. Please believe that. Please understand that and please move on. When I hear you cry for me, the pain hits my heart, and I can't rest. I can't move on myself. And it is not moving on or away from you, but by accepting the fact that I am not on this planet anymore which will allow me to fully experience where I am at. Right now, I am in sort of a crossroad, and it is not where I am truly supposed to be."

"But what do I do without you?" I asked again. Didn't Derrick understand that my life was totally empty now, and there was a void that would never be filled? Didn't he understand that one? Didn't anyone understand that except for myself?

"You will do plenty and achieve a lot of wonderful things without me. You are stronger than you realize, Kit. Just take this one step at a time and move forward with it. Don't stay stuck. If you stay stuck, then so do I."

With that, he was gone again. Not telling me what it was exactly that I was supposed to do or where to begin.

Then I felt a soft breeze that had the hint of gentle spice fragrance, and I heard the wind blow gently past my ear that said, "I just told you now, go do it."

CHAPTER
8

There are seven steps of grief: shock, denial, bargaining, guilt, anger, depression, and acceptance. I think in one week, I went through all six at once. I would go through shock. I would still replay in my mind the minute he was gone, and then guilt would flood in, thinking what I could have done better to make him more comfortable or to help him improve. I would bounce to anger, getting angry at those who still had their loved ones. I would wonder why I was the one left alone. I would bargain with God, that maybe if I would read my Bible with diligence, pray more, or again, if I would work harder, the pain would go away. The pain of losing Derrick at times was unbearable, and I would try to do anything and everything to avoid it. I felt I would never get to acceptance. No! I would never accept his death. I would never move on. Time would have to stand still, and I wanted to keep things the same way as it was before when I had him, which was hard to do especially when his apartment was finally cleaned and emptied and the keys turned over. I would walk by where we lived and try to peer in the patio window. If I looked hard enough, I could see where we had our furniture and remember the laughter and joy we shared in that place. But now it seemed someone else had moved in, and how dare they! It was our place. I was going to finally move in, and I was given the option, but I realized I could not be in that apartment where we both lived. The key word here being *both*.

I felt like I was caught in this web of the seven stages of grief, and in order to find peace of mind, I would have to face up to it all and untangle myself from it and move on. But I wasn't sure if I wanted to. What was Derrick trying to tell me? To move on? From him? But why? Why would I want to move on from him? He was my everything. He made the day sparkle for me whether I was in Paris or Rome or San Francisco. I could e-mail him, text him when I was away. And he would respond and that would give me my lift. No matter how crabby or fussy the passengers were, his daily notes or phone calls gave me what I needed, and I never felt alone.

And then what would I move on to? I didn't see anything in my near future that would motivate me along. My life laid out before me seemed empty and shallow. I had friends, but it didn't seem the same as to have someone like Derrick in my life. I felt like a little lost flight attendant who didn't know where her gate was. I was going from gate to gate, not even knowing the flight number, trying in vain to find my way.

He said to make a list of things to do. What did that mean? Maybe it was to do the things I did when I wasn't with him or to find new things to do to occupy my time. I couldn't remember what I used to do before. I just knew I worked a lot, and when I came home, I got ready for the next trip. But as much as I loved flying and meeting new people, compared to my life with Derrick, it seemed empty. Our short time together, we would hike along the river, go to the theater, the movies, play board games, have dinner parties, and have our own dinner party. There were picnics up with his parents, his siblings, and his family. My days were full and fun. *Now what do I do with them?* I thought to myself. I wasn't sure.

I sat down with an empty page, and I started to make a list of things to do (1) Paint. I used to paint before I started flying and did a lot of canvases for sale. (2) Go hiking (anyway). (3) Learn to dance. (4) Read a book(s). (5) Take a yoga class. (6) Go to church. (7) Volunteer, and then the list started getting silly. I was writing all kinds of stupid and silly activities on the list because my emotions were getting away from me again. I just wasn't sure how I was going to get through this. So I crumpled the list and tossed it against the wall and then got my keys and decided to go for a walk or a coffee shop, just anywhere to get away from this apartment and my grief.

I started to learn that although we can escape grief temporarily, it still follows us until we deal with it head-on. I spent a lot of time running here and there to get away from myself, only to find myself staring straight down and having a wrestling match with grief. Work had to be the only logical answer.

And for a while logging on the hours was my only solution. I did that for two months until I totally exhausted myself. I was burnt out emotionally and physically. I needed to take some time off, and I was able to drop a few trips so I had some time off. But I soon discovered I was back in the same spot. Sitting on the couch and missing my Derrick.

"You are a mess!" the familiar voice said.

I looked up from the couch I was lying on, almost buried underneath a mountain of tissues. It was Derrick. I smiled in relief as it was good to "see" him again. I missed him so much, and to see his ghostly body was better than nothing at this point.

He sat down on a neighboring chair and looked thoughtful as well as stern at me. As if I had done something to really annoy him. "You are just a mess, Kit. Really! What am I going to do with you?" He seemed exasperated with me.

"I don't know," I said weakly. I was still glad to see him and was desperate to run over and hug him, but I knew he was only a ghost and not flesh.

"Kit! I told you to make a list of things to do. You need to get on with life. It's OK to think about me and to think of me fondly—I hope!—but you have to get on with life. Working yourself to death only prolongs the agony, and it does you no good, my dear.

"I told you to make a list of things to do to get yourself back on track. That way you can start focusing on the life you have now and move forward. Remember I told you moving forward does not help you forget about me, but it actually honors me that you are taking what you had with me and using it further to enjoy the rest of your life. You won't forget me, even if you find someone else to share your life with. What we had, no one will ever take away, and what we shared with each other only enhances how wonderful you really are. You have got to stop this silliness and move on."

"I know you are right. But figuring out what to do is hard. I don't know what to do or how to take the first step!" I said earnestly.

"Just do something. I know you liked to paint. Do that. Go to a bookstore and look for hobby books or anything that interests you. Take a trip somewhere. Use that as a launching point. Just do something. Anything even if after a while you don't feel like you are interested in it."

At one point, as I was lying on the couch listening to him, I felt like I was in a therapy session. He was absolutely correct. I had to do something. I had to get out there and not wallow in this apartment or work myself to death.

"You started making a list, but then you gave up. What happened?" he said.

"You were watching me?" I asked. "You can see what I am doing?"

"Every time you weep for me, every time you think of me, every time you go in the depths of despair, as well as anytime you think happy thoughts of me, I can feel it, and I have to see what is going on so I can help you. But you are also keeping me stuck with your tears and your sadness, and I can't move on myself, and I really need to in order to complete the final process of what is the next step with my spirit."

I listened in amazement. In other words, I was not only hurting myself in keeping myself stuck, but I was also hurting him as well.

I sat up, and as I was processing this, he was gone. I wanted to talk to him some more, but it seemed that when I finally understood what he was saying, he would go.

The room became quiet. The chair was empty, and I realized that it was time for me to get refocused and begin to move forward. I went to the bathroom to wash my face. I got the coffee going, and I as I sat down at the table, I began to make a sensible list of things to do, in order to organize my life to move forward. For the first time in a long time, I felt a sense of strength and courage. He was right, I was wasting my life in active grieving. I was past the shock. I was past the disbelief, and I finally felt I was making my way toward acceptance.

CHAPTER
9

I felt a strange wobbly sense of strength. I decided that I was going to get some canvas and begin painting again. I had enjoyed that in the past and had not painted at all when I was with Derrick. I just didn't feel I had the time as we were always busy doing other things, and then when he was ill, I spent my time looking after him.

Buying canvas and paints was a strange experience. When I brought it all home, I felt foolish, like I was kidding myself, but at the same time, it was something I had to do. I wasn't sure what to paint at first, and then I decided to go through some of my old Christmas cards for inspiration. I always enjoyed birds, so I decided to paint cardinals and blue jays as a starter until I felt more inspired.

Sometimes it is hard to take the first step at anything, but I did, and I felt a quiet surge of joy at doing something I hadn't done for a while. The painting kept my focus, and although I was very rusty, I felt like I was moving forward. It had been almost five months since he passed away, and I had spent all this time working and driving myself into the ground, and then endless hours wallowing and diving into self-pity and loneliness. It felt good to be doing something positive.

But despite the fact that the days off were filled with the usual errands and my new hobby, the nights were still hard to endure. Lizzy, my daughter worked most nights. Lizzy actually lived below me in the apartment complex. This way she could watch my apartment when I was gone and collect my mail. She would come down and keep me company when I was home but when she did work the nights were tedious for me. I found myself going up to the cafe for something to eat, but then feeling sad all over again. I wasn't sure how I was going to deal with this. Maybe I would feel like this for the rest of my life. Maybe there was just no getting over Derrick. Painting helped for a short time, but maybe I needed to join an artist group where I could meet new people. Lizzy had suggested going on a singles site online. I wasn't sure about that idea but she went ahead with the plan of hers.

"You have to be kidding!" I said to Lizzy as she had just enrolled me in a dating site. I looked at my profile that she had written, and I couldn't believe she went ahead and did it without me knowing. I was wondering why I was getting notifications on my e-mail from the site that someone winked at me.

"Mom, you need to go out on the weekend. Even if you go out for fun and a night out. You can't be home alone at night, TV, surfing, and holing up in here. You are too young and too vibrant to hide yourself away."

"But I am not interested in meeting anyone," I said becoming annoyed, and in all honesty, a little afraid.

What was I afraid of? Meeting someone new? Replacing Derrick? I couldn't replace him. No way. But I was afraid. I was tired of being by myself on the weekends. My flight attendant friends were working or busy with their own lives. But I felt that going out with someone else would be betraying Derrick.

"I think that is a great idea!" Derrick said. He appeared out of nowhere, standing just next to Lizzy.

"I don't think so!" I said angrily.

"No, it is a good idea. Just go out for coffee or dinner. Have fun. You deserve it. Remember what I said, and that is no one will ever take away what we had, but you are too young and too beautiful to be wasting away on weekends by yourself. I want you to go out and meet others, and just remember, they will never be like me, no one will, because I was always awesome! But you need to find happiness while you are still here. Your story is not done yet. Mine is."

It seemed like there was a three-way conversation going on, with two people in the flesh and one in the spirit. Lizzy could not see Derek standing next to her, and as I was listening to Derrick and trying to answer him, Lizzy was becoming confused and started to have a worried look on her face as if I had gone mad.

"Mom, are you OK?" she said as I had been listening to Derrick instead of answering her.

"I am fine," I said to her. Then I looked at Derrick and said, forgetting Lizzy was standing there hearing me but not hearing Derrick, "I could never love anyone like I loved you. I would be wasting their time. I would be betraying you!"

"Mom?" Lizzy asked, looking concerned.

"Oh, yes!" I said to her as I was trying to recover the conversation. "I will go out ... I will give it a try."

Derrick then said to me, as I turned my face toward him, which was not at Lizzy, "You are not betraying me. I am dead! I am not here! Go ... Lizzy has done you a favor. Get out, have dinner, have some fun! Please!"

I said to Derrick, "OK, but just no, there will never be another you."

"Huh? Mom? I think you need to sit down. Seriously, are you OK?"

"Oh, Lizzy! I am OK, just thinking out loud..." recalling she can't see or hear him. To her, I am just talking to an empty space. "Yes, let's do it!"

"Good!" Derrick said. "I know there will never be another me, I am the best there was out there, but you need to get out and have some fun, Kit. You aren't dead yet. I am! Lizzy did you a favor. Go out ... enjoy. I know you still love or rather loved me. That will never change. Trust me on that. And you aren't betraying me," he added. "You are just moving on with your life. You are honoring me by moving on and not wallowing. I know you loved me ... I know that ... and like I said, I will be waiting for you."

It was a weird thing to be having a conversation with your dead fiancée and your daughter who were all in the same room. Fortunately, before it got more complicated as it already was, he vanished, and it was just Lizzy, and she gently guided me to the couch, thinking that I was having a "moment" with losing my grip on reality. I wasn't. I just couldn't explain to her that Derrick comes to me periodically, and we have "conversations." She would never understand it and think me more daft than she already thought I was.

By the end of the week, I had a date with someone who had seen my profile, and we were going out for a Saturday night coffee, which seemed harmless enough. I was actually excited about it, and it was fun going through the process to get ready for the evening. I bought a new outfit and new makeup. It was nice getting all fussed up for an evening out. I hadn't done this in a long while.

When I got there, Charles was waiting for me, and at first glance, I thought he was very nice-looking indeed. We sat down, both of us nervous and a little bashful, but as we sat down, I immediately wanted to get up and leave. I couldn't go through with this. He wasn't Derrick. He didn't have the same hazel eyes that I loved so much. He didn't have a beard. He didn't have the same look. He was handsome all right, but he had blue eyes. I could never love anyone with blue eyes. This was a mistake. I got through the basic routine conversation of what do you do, what is it like being a flight attendant or a dentist, but he wasn't Derrick. Apparently, Charles liked me enough to want to see me again, but I feigned that I had a trip and wasn't going to be around for the next ten days. That was one thing that was good about being a flight attendant. No one ever really knew where you were. You could get out of a lot of disagreeable things to attend by saying you had to work or had an early show. I could employ this tactic again by saying that I had to work even though I didn't. I didn't give much room for "maybe another time." I just bolted. I felt badly about it as he seemed like a nice and sincere man, but he wasn't Derrick. No one could be him again. He was irreplaceable.

I ran back to my car and burst into floods of tears. I just couldn't do this. I couldn't do anything. Painting had come to a standstill. I was stuck again. I would never get over losing Derrick.

"What happened?" I heard a familiar voice, and there was Derrick in the backseat of my car.

"I just couldn't go through with it," I sobbed.

"Kit. He seemed nice enough. I was lurking, and he seemed to be an OK guy. What happened?"

"He isn't you. He just isn't you. Memories may fade in the shadows, but he just isn't you!"

Derrick, sounding exasperated, said, "Of course, he isn't me! There will never be anyone as wonderful as me, but there will be someone wonderful out there again for you. And you have to realize that. You can't compare them all to me. I am not the ultimate plumb line! I had my faults too! Remember some of those arguments we had?"

"Yes, but I also remember making up."

"Kit, that is not the point. There are a bunch of wonderful men, er well, maybe not as wonderful as me, but wonderful in their own right that you need to meet. You can't go on like this! Please trust the process, Kit. There is life after me! And remember, I will always be a part of you. You have not lost that. We have our memories of wonderful times together, but you need to continue on to make more wonderful memories with someone else. You are too much of a lovely woman, of a person, to be stuck in misery and grief to be by yourself. You have so much love to give, and you have so many more sunny days ahead. You need to go find them, otherwise, you will keep me stuck as I will always have to come back to talk to you to get you going again, and the rest of your life will be nothing but misery. Please move on. Please try again. Please look for love."

With that, he was gone again. I knew he was right. I could still see Charles in the coffee shop window, looking somewhat confused and lonely, but I knew I couldn't go back. I was very rude to him, and there was no way of repairing that mistake. But I also knew that even though Charles may not have been right for me, I would have to continue again, to find myself, and to find that love that would take me through to the end of my story.

CHAPTER
10

I didn't go on any more mystery dates. I wasn't ready to go out and pursue a new relationship. My heart was not into it, and I felt I needed more time as everyone I went out with, I would sit and compare that date to Derrick. It wasn't fair to him, to them, or to me.

Summer was almost over, and October skies were upon us, and I was happy somehow in flying, and when I got home, wrapping myself in my melancholy and painting. I took on painting with a flurry, and I seemed to crank out the canvases as fast as I could buy them. It felt good to paint. I would put on music and then just paint whatever happened. Mostly, it was of birds. Derrick loved birds, and although he never kept one, he enjoyed bird watching, so I concentrated mostly on painting birds. I painted them on boughs of trees, on bird feeders with a fence as backdrop, or I painted a flock of birds flying in an autumn sky or a winter scene of cardinals and blue jays. I found an old photograph and decided to paint a portrait of Derrick for his mother and dad for Christmas. That was the hardest to do of all. Memories of days gone by flooded through my mind, and although I was grateful for the memories, I was also saddened by them. I missed those days gone by. I missed the trips to the grocery store, to the local coffee shop. I missed the mundane things we used to do. I missed doing laundry together. I missed coming home and having him pick me up, or just coming home by myself and coming through the door with my suitcase in tow yelling out a cheery "honey, I am home!" and he would jump up and hug me hello. I missed all that. I thought I would never ever have that again.

Oftentimes I would talk out loud to him. I would say things like "Remember Jennie's wedding? Remember how we danced all night long? You even asked me to dance, and you hated to dance. But we sure did all night long." He never answered back, but I knew he was listening.

"Remember when you first brought me to your mom and dad's home?" I asked aloud one night while I was painting.

"I sure do remember that. I knew they would love you, and love you they did!" I spun around, and it was Derrick. He came back to me again.

"Oh, Derrick. I just miss you so much!" I started to cry. He stood there, as if in real life, smiling at me, but he couldn't reach out to touch me like I am sure he wanted to do. I know I did.

"I miss you too … and you are doing an awesome job painting me. See, I told you to get started on something."

"Well, I kind of missed painting actually. And I am glad you like your portrait."

Derrick smiled and said, "I love it. You have totally captured me with your oils. I am amazed."

"I painted it with my heart. I know that sounds cliché, but I stand here and think of you and all the wonderful times we had and how I miss you so much, and it just comes right out here on the canvas. I plan on giving this to your parents," I said.

"They will love it. Just as much as they love you." Derrick walked around and examined the other canvases I had painted, and he said, "You really do good work. Have you ever thought of exhibiting some of these?"

I shook my head. "I don't think I am that good enough," I said.

"You will never know unless you try." Derrick looked at me thoughtfully. He was always the one to encourage me. When I had a tough trip with difficult passengers or crew members, he was always the one to make things better again.

"I know … maybe I will give it a shot but not until I have enough to show a jury." I sat down and looked at Derrick and said,

"Would you come back to me? Even if you were coming to me as a ghost, would you come back to me at least until it was my time?" I thought how much more bearable my life would be if he could do that. If he could pop in and out, and we could have these moments where at least I could see his vision, and we could talk.

He sadly shook his head. "No, I am only here for a short time to see you get through this ordeal. And don't think you can stretch it out by not helping yourself either, young lady!" He gently wagged his finger at me. "You have to really try to move on because without you moving on, I really can't. And if I am told that there is no progress being made, I won't be able to come down to keep motivating you, and you will still be stuck in your grief, will have missed out on so much. I want to help you, but you have to start helping yourself."

"But my heart aches for you. Every time I hear a song or go to a place we once went to, I start to hurt all over again. I can't shake this. I loved you so much." I started to cry again. How much longer could I bear the pain of missing him? Painting helped, but all that did for me was pile a collection of canvasses that I had no clue with what to do. How many more paintings could I do that would help ease the pain?

Derrick looked at me and said, "I know, but you simply have to really go full throttle and move on. It doesn't mean in particular a new relationship but to just get on with life and other people. Hibernating yourself in the apartment every time you have off and painting is a start ... Well, it is a start, painting, but you need to get out again with people and enjoy your life."

"How can I really enjoy life when there is no you?" I said sadly.

And then he was gone again.

I collapsed onto the couch and just started to cry. I was grateful Lizzy was gone for the evening as she was even getting tired of me, but I couldn't stop crying, and I cried until I fell asleep.

Lizzy came home later that night to check on me and found me on the couch. She woke me up, and I came too, surprised I had fallen hard asleep. It was strange, but the mix of crying and sleeping had a profound effect on me.

"Mom, are you going to be OK?" she asked gently. "Mom, you do manage to go to work, and you do manage to apply yourself to your painting, and you are doing an awesome job, but I am worried about you."

"I'm OK," I lied.

"No, you aren't. Either you need to get some therapy counseling, or you need to snap out of this right away. You aren't doing yourself any favor. I need you! I need you not to fall apart on me." Lizzy looked at me, pleading with her big brown eyes. What an endearing girl to be mother to.

"I think I will be OK. I know I need to get a grip on myself. I know things will never be the same again. I know that Derrick is gone, and everything has been altered. And I know I need to find my purpose in life again."

I sat up as Lizzy brought me a cup of tea, and she sat with me as I drank it.

"Mom, I think you need to do a collection of your paintings and have it juried. Have someone look at it and see if you can have an exposition somewhere. You have an enormous amount of talent, and you need to pour that into your paintings. You are an awesome flight attendant, but you have so much more to give. Derrick would want it that way. I know he would. He would want you to dive into your paintings and make something out of it. He would not want you to sit and brood about him all the time. I think that would only upset him even more," Lizzy said it to me with so much conviction that I felt she knew something.

"I know you are right," I said, feeling resigned. "Next spring, I will take my collection to Frederick's, you know, the art dealer in Minneapolis and see what he thinks."

"I know what he will think, Mom. He will tell you that he will sign you up for his summer show."

"Then, that is what I will do. I will finish this piece and give it to Mom and Dad, and then start on a new collection of birds ... , and I will see where that takes me. And if it doesn't take me anywhere, at least I have been doing something with a possible goal in mind."

"That is it!" Lizzy smiled. "And go out with people. Join an art group, or answer some of those messages on the over-forty group, and just go for coffee. You don't have to marry them, Mom. Just go and do. Get a few new outfits and dress up and just go. Mom, there will never be another Derrick. Derrick was a lovely man. You and him were perfect together, but you know he did have his faults too. He was always late, you even said that if you wanted to go out or go on a trip, that you would have to tell him an hour before the program or trip what time to leave. He always wore those baggy jeans that never fit in the bottom."

"Wait a minute!" It was Derrick's voice, and then he began to materialize. Derrick apparently was listening and was interrupting.

"Be quiet!" I said to him.

Lizzy looked startled. "I'm sorry, Mom!"

"No, it's not you, it's … ah … well, never mind," I said looking at Derrick who was looking with a mock expression of annoyance at Lizzy's remark. "You both are right, er, I mean you are right, Liz. I don't have to marry them, I can just go out for coffee and conversation. No harm done. And I will get on with those paintings. Even though nothing may ever come out of it, at least I am focused on a goal."

"That is the point, Mom. You need to be focused on a goal, a project, something to get you to start moving forward. While you are dealing with your own emotions, you can pour some of that energy into something positive. Derrick would want that. I know he would. And please get out and meet people. Join a group, a friendship site, something, anything so that you can get involved with life again. You have to, otherwise you will emotionally disintegrate, and I need you, Mom. I need you to be here for me, and you should understand that you still have most of your life to live. Derrick was a wonderful man, and you will never find another him, but in the same vein, there are other wonderful people out there to get to know, to be friends with, and to love."

I almost started to cry. I knew Lizzy was right and how did she get to be so smart in such a short time?

"All right. I will keep up with the paintings, and I will explore places to make friends and get out more often."

I hugged her and thought how lucky I was to have her as my daughter. As I brushed back a tear, I said, "I promise."

And in that split moment, I heard a voice in the back whisper, "Atta, girl." I spun around in the direction of the voice and saw him briefly wink at me, and then he was gone.

CHAPTER
11

The snow outside my retirement apartment was falling more heavily now and was piling up. It was later in the afternoon, and it seemed like rooms were getting colder. I reached for my lap blanket and tucked it in around me. I was glad I was safe inside and not having to deal with snow issues anymore. I closed my eyes and thought back fondly of the many times I brushed the snow off Derrick's car before he went to work, or the times we went coasting down the big hill near the house. We would end up in a happy tumble and then retreat to the house to warm up with a cup of Baileys and cocoa while cooking up a pot of chicken soup. Those were wonderful days. Alan enjoyed the snow as well, and I have to say we had lovely times too, as we would actually go to a resort and go snowmobiling and cross-country skiing up north. It was exhilarating and fun to sit by the fire and warm up again with a hot drink. I was blessed that I had the love of two fine men in my life, and I miss them both equally. But after Alan died two years ago, he never reappeared like Derrick did. What was the difference? I don't know, but I do know that if Derrick hadn't come back to help me, I might have died years ago, with a broken heart and talents undiscovered.

As I close my eyes, I look back again to that time in my life when things were falling apart.

"Mrs. Brinkley?" a voice said in the crack of my door, breaking my reverie.

"Yes?" It was Augusta who was one of the caregivers at the assisted-living facility.

Augusta came in and gave me my medication, which I took willingly, and then asked me if I wanted dinner in my room or at the dining hall. I wanted to be alone with my thoughts and dreams, and I requested dinner in my room. I just didn't feel like socializing at the moment. I wanted to be alone, I told her.

She quietly left, and I went back to my thoughts and memories.

Oh, yes! I thought to myself and closed my eyes and drifted back in time.

I remember signing up for clubs and friendship groups. It was hard at first. I was a flight attendant, and my schedule could be variable at times. But I managed to find an over-forties friendship group that went out to dinner at a local restaurant every Thursday night. There were ten of us, and I remember that one of the members was a nice-looking man who just lost his wife.

"Hi! My name is Katherine, but people call me Kit!" I said as I shook his hand that first night at dinner.

"Hi, I'm Alan!" he said as we happened to sit down next to each other.

We started exchanging that usual bit of information in between ordering and talking to others that either sat across from us or next to us. Alan seemed like a nice man, and we got along. Strangely enough, his wife had died three months prior and was struggling emotionally like I was. But he seemed to be having more of a harder time with the loss than I did, if that was even possible.

I was enjoying the Thursday-night dinners when I would be in town, and I was starting to enjoy meeting some of the other people that would come. I kept my social activities to that because being a flight attendant did take up time as well as painting. When I would come home from a trip, I would be mentally and physically exhausted, and I was grateful for that because I still remembered the feeling of coming to the passenger pickup and seeing Derrick waiting for me to give me "princess parking," which was a phrase used by us sky people to mean that someone was picking me up. After collapsing into a heap and then getting out of my uniform, I would rest a bit and then dive into my painting. If it was a Thursday night, I would rest up and get ready to go out to dinner with my group. All this was keeping me focused and going, but in between the cracks of space of time, I would feel a little pain of missing my Derrick.

Christmas was coming, as evident of all the holiday decorations in the stores and the streetlights. I knew this was going to be hard for me as all the lights and the snow and the happy sounds reminded me of last Christmas and the one before. Despite his illness, we were hopeful for the future, and all I wanted was to be with Derrick and try to make merry as best we could, and we did. It was one of the nicest Christmases I had, but this was going to be the first one without him, and it was going to be hard.

I had an invitation from his parents to go up to Eagles Mere with the rest of the family. Lizzy was invited as well. I thought about it seriously and wondered if just being home alone or planning to work would be a better idea, but Lizzy convinced me that I needed to be with family, even if it was his. They invited me, so I accepted.

The portrait was almost finished as I had been working diligently on it. It was coming to life, and at times, it made me sad, and then at other times, it gave me such a great comfort to look at it. I wasn't even sure I could give it up, but I knew I had to. His parents would love hanging it in the foyer.

It was two weeks before Christmas when Alan, after helping me with my coat at our group dinner, asked me if I would be his date at his office Christmas party. I said sure and then realized I had to scramble for a dress. I didn't have any cocktail party dress, and this meant a mad scramble to the mall to get something to wear. I had to get the help of Lizzy, which she was happy to help.

"So who is this Alan, Mom? Hmmmm?" She looked at me slyly as if I was keeping a great secret.

"Oh, he is just a person I met in my Thursday-night dinner group," I said somewhat embarrassed. "He is just a friend, nothing more."

"That is what they all say!" she said as she got her keys to the car, and going out the door, I told her to quit teasing me. She just laughed!

It wasn't easy picking out a dress. The price wasn't an issue. Well, yes, it was actually. But I didn't want anything dowdy and plain, but at the same time, I didn't want to come on like a siren and give Alan mixed messages.

In the dressing room, I slipped on a dark-blue chiffon dress with a low neckline with a lot of bling at the waistline. There was a little bit of saucy sash at the side that would float whenever I walked. I stood in front of the mirror and wondered if this was the right dress for me. I loved it, but again, I didn't want to come on too strong. The other option was a black cocktail dress with a high-scoop neckline and capped sleeves.

"You look stunning."

As I heard the voice, I turned around to see where it came from, and it was Derrick admiring me.

"Buy it!" he said.

"Are you kidding! It's $125! I can't afford that on my salary!"

"You only live once!" Derrick said with a slight chuckle. "I should know that better than anyone, I suppose!"

"Ha-ha!" I said in a mocking tone.

"Can I help you?" It was the clerk who saw me standing in front of the mirror.

"I am not sure! I may be way beyond help!" I said looking at Derrick, who was smiling at me. "I think I may take this dress." I finally resigned to the fact that it was a beautiful dress, and I was going to buy it for me, and for Derrick. For Derrick. I mused to myself. He is dead, and I am buying a dress because he says I look hot in it. How strange is that?

The clerk smiled and looked at me strangely, and why should she not look at me strangely? I was in her eyes talking to myself. My daughter was off in another department looking for outfits for herself.

"Very well then, I can help you check out," she said and smiled and went her way, and I could see her shaking her head, probably thinking me as very odd.

As she left, my daughter came back and saw me in the dress, and her jaw dropped.

"Mom, you look gorgeous. I hope you are going to settle on that one. The other black made you look like a librarian," she said.

"I totally agree with her." Derrick was still there smiling at me.

"Well, it is expensive, but I guess I am going to take it," I said, not sure if indeed I was going crazy. Not for just talking to apparitions, but for spending such a large sum of money on a dress I might only wear once, and for going out with a man that I just met a few weeks ago that I had no interest in other than being friends.

I paid for the dress and then walked out feeling weak-kneed but excited at the same time. How quickly things had changed. Last winter I was coming home to Derrick who was ill, but yet still had some amount of energy to enjoy holiday fun, and now this winter, I was without him and going out with a man I really didn't know that well. How quickly things can change.

CHAPTER
12

Saturday night came, and I found myself in the middle of a hotel ballroom, bedecked in holiday lights and a live band. Tables had white linen and a beautiful pine garland with a red candle-lit hurricane glass cover. The room was literally in a glow of diamond sparkles, and I was enchanted by it all.

Alan, who normally came to the dinners in a sweater and jeans, looked beyond handsome in a black suit and tie. He looked so polished and smart, and I was dazzled by him. He was a handsome man anyway. He was just turning gray around the edges, and with this sharp, chiseled look, he was indeed a head turner. His brown eyes twinkled at me, and as we found our way to the dance floor, he held me close as we went around the dance floor. I could smell his soap and aftershave, and the warmth of his cheek pressed next to mine was scratchy, but at the same time, it felt good.

He pulled slightly apart from me and said, "Kit, you look beautiful tonight. That dress is gorgeous, and everything about you is stunning. I love what you did with your hair."

"You can thank Lizzy. She knows how to french braid." My thoughts went back to getting ready for Alan's arrival. I was way beyond nervous as it was the first time I went out with anyone formally. I was also confused because for the first time, despite the fact I was nervous, I was also excited to be going out. It really did feel good to get all dressed up for an occasion, and I was generally excited for the evening to begin.

"Sit still!" Lizzy commanded. "You are jerking around too much," she said as she was trying to get a tight french braid going down the back.

"Do you think putting some of these snowflake clips would be OK in alternating spots of the braid?" I asked. I handed her some tiny snowflake hair clips that I bought later on that day we were at the mall. After spending money on a dress, I realized I needed shoes and hair accessories and makeup and a new purse. It was getting out of hand, but for the first time, it was a lot of fun to be shopping for something as exciting as a Christmas party. I wasn't sure what was coming over me, but I felt as light as a feather that afternoon after I got over the initial shock of the dress and thinking I would have to eat ramen noodles in January to make up for all of this.

"I think that would look great," she agreed.

She put the finishing touches on my hair and then put on my makeup. Then I carefully slipped into my dress and the new pumps I bought to go along with the dress. The blue clutch purse pulled everything together.

"Let me see you!" Lizzy said as she inspected the hair, the makeup, and the dress." She looked at me thoughtfully and then started to well up and say, "Mom, you look beautiful."

Pulling out of the memory of getting ready, Alan pulled me back to real time and said, "You look beautiful. I can't believe I am with a beautiful lady such as you."

He kissed me slightly on the cheek as we were dancing as I looked over his shoulder to see Derrick standing in the middle of the crowd nodding his approval. At that moment, I felt torn, and I wanted this all to be different. I wanted Alan to be Derrick. I wanted to be dancing with Derrick, not Alan. I began to panic, thinking I could never love anyone ever again, and what I was doing with Alan, who was giving me the time of my life, but at the same time, I wanted my time to be with Derrick. I immediately pulled away and excused myself.

"Did I say something wrong to upset you?" Alan asked as he went after me, but I was too fast for him even in my pumps.

'No!" I said as I weaved my way through the crowd. "I am just having a moment!" He stopped following me, and for that split second, I wished he would have followed me.

I made my way to the ladies' lounge where I started to cry. I closed my eyes, and my heart ached beyond anything I ever felt before. I wanted Derrick back. I wanted to go home. I wanted to just fade away somewhere.

"Honey, are you OK?" asked a woman in the lounge. She went and gave me a tissue. "Is there anything I can do?"

"No, I am OK," I sniffed back. "I just need a minute."

"Alright then," she said apprehensively.

I sat down on the plush bench and tried to pull myself together. It wasn't fair to Alan to fall apart like this as this was such a lovely evening. It wasn't fair to him to spoil it. He did nothing wrong. I just couldn't let go.

It was then I saw Derrick. He was standing before me.

"Why did you come here?" I sniffed.

"I don't know, I just had to see you again. You look so beautiful, and I wanted to take you in. It was wrong for me to come, I am sure I will hear it when I go back." He sighed. "But you look so beautiful and so comfortable with Alan. I can't help you anymore. You know what to do, you know how to cope, but you looked so beautiful, I just had to come back one more time."

"What do you mean, Derrick?"

"It is just that. My time here trying to help you move forward is done. You have done a great job … your work, your paintings, your involvement with Life. That is where you need to be, you need to be with Life. I just wanted to see you one more time. I wanted to take you in, and you are amazing, especially the way you look tonight."

I realized that this was going to be the last encounter with Derrick. I felt panicked and wanted to say something that would make him keep coming back. But for the first time, he looked very sad and resigned.

"I need you!"

"No, you don't. Alan does. Alan needs you, and I think he is falling in love with you. He is alive, Kit, he is alive. Remember I am not. I was only here for a short period to get you back on track, and you are getting there. You will still miss me from time to time. You won't forget me, and every time you think of me, I will feel it and will smile. It doesn't bother me that you are with someone else… well, maybe just a little bit, but I know that my story is done, and you have so much love to give, you can't waste it on a dead man. Give it to someone who is living. Go out to him. Go out and live and love and enjoy the rest of your life, Kit. You deserve it!"

"What will I ever do?" I said sadly. "What will I do without you?"

"Kit, you are without me. I am dead. I am gone… but I am not far away. And you are doing just fine, Kit. You are discovering things about yourself that you never knew. You are finding strength that you never thought you possessed. You are doing fine! Trust me, trust the process. I will be waiting."

And he was gone.

Everything seemed to be going on around me. Music, laughter, ladies coming in and out of the lounge, it came back into focus, and for a moment, I tried to process all that was said, and I knew I had to do something in a minute; otherwise, I would lose something again that I may never be able to find again.

I dried my eyes and touched up my makeup and then left the lounge only to see Alan looking very worried and frantic.

"What is wrong, Kit? What did I do?" Alan said with worried eyes and expression.

"I am OK. I just had a moment. It's hard to explain," I said.

He took me to an enclosed patio. The snow was falling softly outside, making the entire night magical.

We sat down, and he took my hands and said, "Ever since I met you, I thought I was going to be given a second chance. Susan, my wife, well, she was my soul mate. And I felt like I could never find anyone like her again. Until I saw you. You are full of enthusiasm and energy, and I was so happy to have met you.

"I actually didn't want to meet anyone or care to meet anyone. I was just happy to sit at home and read the paper and watch TV. But my friend encouraged me to join a group and get out. So I signed up for these Thursday-night dinners, and when you came in, when you joined, I was taken away by you. I sorta felt guilty, like I was betraying my Susan, but at the same time, I think she would want me to move on. It is not that I don't love her, it is that there are other loves out there that are unique unto themselves. And I was hoping it would be you. I want it to be you."

It was like he and I had led parallel lives. He with his Susan and me with my Derrick. I wanted to ask him if she haunted him like my Derrick did, but then I thought I better not go there. It was even too much for me to believe at times.

"I am sorry if I hurt you in any way," he said looking sad and almost hopeless that he had single-handedly ruined the evening.

"No, you didn't!" I said as I took his hands in mine. "I am having a splendid evening. I just had a collision in my mind. It is hard to explain, but a lot of thoughts and emotions were overtaking me." I smiled as I tried to explain why I dashed out so quickly. I couldn't tell him "well, I saw my dead fiancée."

"I think I can understand," Alan said quietly. "I heard from Maddy, the organizer, that you recently lost someone too. And it is not easy. But I am finding with you, that I can finally find a reason to live. And I want to get to know you more, Kit. Please say that will happen."

I smiled at him, and I said, "I reckon so."

"Then let's go back to the party. I'm hungry, and the buffet looks really good," he said.

I looked at him and saw that even though he wasn't Derrick, nor would he ever be, maybe there really was happiness after such a tragic sorrow, and maybe he was right. We could both find a reason to live and truly move on.

As he took my arm, we walked back to our table, and we both decided to skip the dancing and head on to the buffet. I wasn't expecting it, but Derrick was there behind the pillar next to the buffet table. I saw him, but I wasn't going to let it upset me anymore. He was just watching me and smiling as if he approved.

As I walked closer to the buffet table trying to keep my attention on Alan, I saw Derrick mouth "atta, girl," and then say "I will always love you...and I will be waiting." I smiled over at him, and then he was gone. And I knew he was really gone for good.

CHAPTER
13

I didn't want the night to end. We laughed and danced, and we closed the place down. I felt light and happy for the first time in a long time. And to think I went out just for a night out, something to do. It was indeed magical. I didn't want it to end. But it was time to go home, and we drove home in silence. Not an angry or awkward silence but a contented silence, and he took my hand and gave it a quick squeeze to reassure me that even though he was driving and concentrating on the snowy roads, he was thinking of me.

He took me home, but he didn't come in. He kissed me passionately in the car and said, "I will walk you to the door, but there is where I will leave you. But I will call you, and we'll go out for dinner ... and not with the Thursday night group but some place fine."

I floated through the door and to my apartment. I had a hard time calming down as I felt that somehow I had gotten over a very large hurdle in my life. Was I at acceptance? I pulled out a photograph of Derrick and the last fine time we had. It was strange. But as I looked at it, it didn't haunt me like the photos used to. Suddenly remembering him and those wonderful times I had with him really didn't make me feel overwhelmed and sad. I didn't want another relationship, but here I found myself starting a new one. How strange was that? And I was supposed to be going to Derrick's mom and dad's place for Christmas? How would that be? Would they be able to tell that I was involved with someone else? Would it matter? I would find out in a few weeks.

I didn't want to take my dress off as it would signal the end of a beautiful evening, but I was getting tired and needed to go to bed. But I knew that even though I was tired, my head was too light to set it down. However, I knew that if I didn't even try to go to sleep, I would hate myself in the morning, and my entire day would be consumed in a nap. I had too much to do, like get ready for the next trip and get my paintings ready.

I finally took off the magical dress and was glad I did spend the money on it. I put it away back in the dress bag and then put on my lounge pants and T-shirt and fell asleep. Lizzy would want to know all about the day, and she would wake me up early enough to get the details, so I gave into sleep and enjoyed sweet dreams inspired by Alan and the night that was spent with him.

I was expecting a call from him the next day or a text or something. I did text him but no reply. I figured he was just as tired as I was and was sleeping or just resting. But the next day and thereafter, there was no message or call from him, and I was getting worried and concerned. I had sent out a few texts that day, but there was nothing. I was becoming upset and at one point thought it was because of my meltdown. Christmas was soon here, and I was even thinking of getting him a small gift. He wasn't at the following Thursday-night dinners, and I was becoming more upset. I had given up texting him and figured it was just over. Like everything else in my life.

Christmas Eve morning, Lizzy and I were getting ready to pack a few things to go up to Eagles Mere to spend the two days over Christmas. I had just finished the portrait of Derrick and was going to give it as a gift to his mom and dad.

We were just getting ready to leave for Eagles Mere when my phone rang. It was Alan. I wasn't going to answer it as I was really upset with him for not returning texts or phone calls and wasn't really sure how to handle the situation.

"Well, look who is finally going to talk to me!" I was really annoyed. "What happened? What did I do?"

"Kit! I am so sorry! But I had to fly to England on a project, and I don't have international calling, and I didn't want to tell you anything because I had a lot on my mind, a lot to do, and a surprise."

"What a great excuse!" I said in an annoyed tone.

"No, I am serious. Kit, I have good news for you."

"What? And make it snappy as I am about to leave town for two days."

"Kit. Remember you showed me those paintings?"

"Yeah!" I said not wishing to talk anymore but to get on the road.

"Well, I can get you a showing of your paintings. I have a few people who are interested in your work," he said excitedly. I have a few friends in the art world, and I ran into them at the Savoy and showed them some of the photos that you gave me when we first met, and they really like your work. If you want to have a collection ready by March, we really can get you out there in the art world."

"You know personally Frederick's, the art dealer and house in Minneapolis?" I asked. I felt my stomach move down to my toes. I began to tremble. I wasn't sure if this was really happening to me.

"No better yet. Lloyd's of Chicago Art Gallery which is one of the top ones in the nation. Kit, you have talent. Even though you paint birds, you show a lot of passion, intensity, and movement. When people paint birds, they just paint with a two-dimensional attitude. You pour everything you have in your work. And the portrait you were working on, they want to see it too."

"You gotta be kidding!" I said, still in a mild state of shock and joy.

"No, I am not. I am so sorry I wasn't able to contact you till now, but I was busy with Mr. Lloyd himself, and he is very interested in you. He was actually in London with me last week. My friends introduced me to him at a party, and we had dinner. I wanted this to be a surprise."

"It sure is!" I said. I wasn't sure what to say or do. "But you told me you were an engineer ... You were an architect."

"I am, but I do have some friends who have connections with the art world. I just don't talk a lot about it. I guess I should have told you. But when you told me you paint on the side, I thought 'OK, let's see what you do.' And I was amazed at your work. You have a lot of talent, girl. What are you doing flying?"

"That is a good question!" I said "Well, OK … When do you need the canvases, and how many do you need?"

"I need all you have plus the portrait. It's finished, isn't it?"

"Yes, it is. But I was going to give it as a gift."

"Can you delay the gift giving for a couple of months? Tell them it is going to be in a showing."

"Sure, but I can't sell it!"

"No worries," Alan said. "Look, go on with your Christmas holidays, and can I see you when you get back? And mind you, I meant it then, I mean it now. Call me when you get back, and if you aren't flying, then let's go out. And, Kit, you have been on my mind. I just wasn't able to call you. I was so busy with all of this, and with my own stuff. I know I should have responded, but I wanted to be sure that we secured a showing for you, and I wanted to surprise you for Christmas."

"Well, you sure did," I replied, still unable to take it all in.

"Call me when you get back … and if I can call you at Christmas…"

"Sure, sure … I would really like that."

"I will do that then. Merry Christmas, and, Kit, I am hoping that next Christmas I will be spending it with you."

"I kinda hope that too!" I said shyly.

We hung up, and I looked at Lizzy as if I really were a deer in the headlights.

"What is going on, Mom?" she asked me expectantly.

"I will tell you in the car, but you are driving!" I said. "Let's get going!"

CHAPTER
14

It was strange going back to the home where Derrick and I shared many memories together. My thoughts kept floating back to last Christmas when he was ill and then the Christmas before that and how happy we had been. It was great to see everyone again and all the cousins as well as the grandchildren. There was a flurry of excitement that was contagious. Wonderful Christmas smells of cookies and turkey and baked yams, corn soufflé, and other traditional Christmas foods were being prepared. It was a lot to take in, but I was glad to be here.

I was ushered up into the old room where we shared, and it was strange being there by myself. Lizzy was going to be across the hall. The room seemed empty, and as I sat down in the chair, I thought of how we unpacked and got dressed for dinner, going down the great staircase together dressed in our Christmas finery. Chaos going on down below, we would grab some treats that were on the buffet table and then head to the library where we could at least hear ourselves think. The memory of the laughter that came between the two of us came flooding back, and I wasn't sure if I wanted to laugh or to cry. I felt caught in between two emotions all at once. I leaned my head back, thinking of all of those memories.

"I don't know if I am brave enough to go down!" Derrick said with a smile.

"I know, there are a lot of kids just flying around. I think if we do go downstairs, we will be taking our lives into our own hands!"

"I know what you mean. There are kids everywhere... I am beginning to wonder if they all belong to the family or if Mom recruited more from the neighbors!" Derrick laughed.

"Well, we will have to go down sometime, otherwise they will wonder about us."

"I think they already do!" Derrick smiled. "Come on. At least let's go downstairs and get something to eat."

"Good idea."

"Mom?" It was Lizzy peeking her head into my room. "Are you coming down?" she asked.

"Yeah. I was just thinking to myself."

"I know, Mom, it's hard, but Derrick would be really happy that you were spending the holidays here."

"I know. I do miss him, Lizzy. And I am so confused... Alan, Derrick. I don't know."

"Alan is alive... Derrick would want you to go on with your life. He wouldn't want you to be putting yourself on the shelf. Mom, it will be OK. Let's go downstairs and enjoy the fun. There is a game of hearts going on in the library. Maybe we can get in on that."

Lizzy convinced me to get moving, and so I did. As I walked around the rooms, I felt like I was a part of the group, but at the same time, distant from everyone. Everyone was laughing and enjoying themselves. Children were running around and chasing. Clusters of cousins were around tables or congregated in the living room area talking about this or that. If Derek were alive, I would have felt more a part of the group, but although the family invitation was sincere, I still felt like I was in between it all. And I wasn't sure where I fit in or if I did fit in anymore. They say blood is thicker than water, and at times, I felt like I was still a part of the family, I knew I wasn't. It was evident here and now.

Lizzy wasn't having the same problem as I was. She was in the library watching a game of hearts being played and eyeing Colin, one of Derrick's nephews, and when she found the right time, slipped next to him at the table and joined in as she had planned. He seemed taken with her, and I wondered if this was the beginning of something big. I peeked in the room and watched them laugh and slap cards down on the table and then a huge groan of sighs when someone got the queen of spades. More laughter and more playing of cards and more elbow pokes and sighs when someone got a handful of hearts.

"Remember when we used to play?" I looked around, and there he was. Derrick. He had come back for Christmas Eve.

"What are you doing here? I thought you were going to not come back ever again. Not that I don't want you to leave, but I thought you had to move on as well?" I had walked to an area where I wouldn't look foolish appearing to be talking to myself.

"I had to come back as I could feel you thinking of me again tonight. We had fun here, didn't we?"

"Yes, we did, and that is why it is so hard, especially tonight. We could have had more Christmases together." The tears were starting to well up in my eyes. I really couldn't stand to be here any longer. Lizzy was having a fun time, but I was not. There was too much happiness in these rooms, and I felt very much left out in all of it. I wanted to laugh again like everyone else was. Didn't they understand that they were missing a family member tonight?

"My dear Kit, life has to go on. My family does miss me, especially Mom. I can feel it from her too. My family is trying to make it a nice holiday for each other, and they are doing a good job. I am not hurt by it at all. I am happy that everyone seems to be pulling it together at least for the littles. But I keep telling you, don't feel sad tonight. Just be glad of the time we had together. It will always be special, and you will always remember it. But from what I understand, you have someone who really likes you in your life, and you need to pursue that. I am not offended or put out. He is alive. I am not! You need to move on."

"I know, but he isn't you. He isn't you. I will always be afraid I will be comparing him to you."

"No, you won't. You won't do that because he will make you laugh and smile again. Please, Kit, just trust the process. Let someone else love you, let someone else be with you and make you smile. I shouldn't have come to upset you, but I just wanted to talk to you one last time … I guess I miss you too … but I ask you, Kit, enjoy the day, enjoy the holiday, enjoy my family, and you will be able to smile again."

With that he was gone again. And I felt a huge sense of relief from my shoulders. Was it just seeing him again, or was it what he said? He really did want me to move on. He was serious this time.

I pulled out my phone and texted Alan.

Merry Christmas, Alan

A text came back shortly thereafter.

Same to you. Will see you soon, Kit!

I felt more relaxed and was able to join in and not feel like I was a third wheel. The Christmas Eve dinner was served, and everything tasted and smelled good. The table looked festive and elegant. It couldn't have been any nicer. Christmas prayers were said, and then a moment of silence for Derrick to which my eyes filled with tears, but then unbeknownst to myself, everyone else was teary-eyed. After that moment, I could hear people bring out their hankies or deftly wipe their eyes so that it was not noticed. My gaze went over to the corner of the room, and there he was again. He was right there in the corner watching us. I smiled, and he gave me the thumbs-up, and then he was gone.

CHAPTER
15

After dinner and the dishes and the food were quickly put away, it was time to open presents. The kids could not hold out any longer, and neither could the young adults it seemed. Lizzy took her place next to Colin, and the younger kids acted as Santa giving out a present to everyone there, and then we would open it at once.

The last present was my portrait of Derrick I had just finished. I came back from the library where I had it in the closet, and when I brought it up, I knew that Mom was expecting it. I came over to his parents, and I made an announcement.

Clearing my throat, I said, "I had picked up my old hobby of painting and had been painting not only birds, but I had done a portrait of Derrick for you to have. However, I have been invited to a showing in March where not only my birds will be presented, but the portrait of Derrick will be featured."

I unveiled it, and there was a huge gasp in the room. Cynthia and Douglas, or Mom and Dad as I had affectionately started to call them, began to cry, and you could hear a pin drop in the room. My heart lurched, and I panicked, thinking that they hated it. "Well, what do you think?" I asked nervously.

Mom could hardly talk, but then she said, "It is the most amazing portrait I have ever seen. You captured him brilliantly." Everyone else agreed. Mom then came over to me and gave me a hug and kiss and said she would be pleased as ever to hang it in the hall after the showing.

She grabbed both my hands and said, "You have the most amazing talent that I didn't know you possessed. I am sure you will get rave reviews for Derrick's picture." Everyone else agreed and then circled around me asking me if I could paint their child's portrait and how much would I charge. I was flattered and taken aback, and it took me to go back into my room to process this all. It was too flattering sweet to be true, and that was the best Christmas gift I had yet to receive.

The next day was spent relaxing and visiting with family. I had wanted to get home as I felt inspired by all the positive feedback regarding my painting. I decided to leave later Christmas evening, and I soon realized after Lizzy's endless prattle in the car about Colin that maybe I would always have a tie to this family, if not through Lizzy.

But although the holiday week to New Year's was just getting underway, I had to go back to work and fly the trips that were assigned to me. However, I could not wait to get back and get organized on other pieces of work that I had agreed to do.

Luckily, I had New Year's Eve off, and I agreed to go out with Alan, although we were going to be spending it at his place as we both did not like that craziness that was all about New Year's. We decided to invite a few friends over, mostly his, for dinner and celebrate playing games or socializing.

I felt comfortable with Alan, and there were times I did forget about Derrick. Alan had me laughing and smiling in a new way, and I felt like all the grief and the tugs at the heart could finally be behind me. I realized that it never truly was because there would be a song that would be playing that would trigger an emotion, or a Friday night would go by, and I would think about what Derrick and I would do to get ready for the weekend. Going to the theater sometimes triggered an emotion, but I quickly put it at bay, realizing that this was what Derrick wanted me to do. I was falling in love with Alan.

At the stroke of midnight in New York, we watched the ball drop. For me that was the official start of the New Year. Alan turned toward me and then kissed me and then said, "Happy New Year,

Kit. I hope this is the start of many happy new years to come." With that, I knew that this was the beginning of my new life, and with the prospect of a showing in March, orders for portraits to be done, I could feel the sadness of the year past melt away and the promise of something new and exciting to begin. I thought briefly of Derrick. How could I not? But I also felt and understood that he was happy for me in my happiness, and he knew that even though I found a new love, I would always have the old one tucked away in my heart.

I was glad for the prospect of having a showing coming up in March. As much as Alan and I were getting along very well, still the anniversary of Derrick's death was coming up. I wasn't sure how I was going to react. Do I sit and think about him all day? Do I get on with things? Do I light a candle in his memory? I wasn't sure what I should do. Until I realized that the day of the showing was the actual anniversary of his death. I knew until then I had to keep busy and focused on my job of flying and my finishing up some last-minute paintings. It is funny how one thing leads to another. I always did like painting but never took myself seriously as a painter. I used to do the odd canvases, but when I started flying, I forgot all about my painting. It took Derrick to leave me to discover I had a burning talent within and to get me to the place that I was now headed. I would have rather had Derrick than discovering that I could do well with my paintings, but it is what grief brought out, and it helped me to survive the rough and unsteady road of his passing. I had to reach outside of the box in my grief to come to the realization that I could paint, and it would delight so many people. To be in a show was incredible. I never dreamed it would happen to me, but in a few months, it was going to happen, and hopefully it would be a success.

I had appointments for the cousins to come and sit for their portrait, but until then, I was doing some things on my own, and surprisingly enough, I was taken by sunsets and sunrises from the view from the top. I started a few sunrise paintings from my early morning flights, and in some ways, it was reflective of my soul and how I was beginning to feel. It was like I was being reborn. Either by the friendship and companionship of Alan and my new budding career as a painter. I especially liked to do the sunrises with the sea as a backdrop. They sparked a whole new interest within my muse. The sunrise across the ocean seemed magical and mystical, and I could paint into the night working on a boundless energy I never thought I had.

And this was the only beginning of the year. Although it marked the first anniversary of Derrick's departure from this earth, it also marked a new beginning of my career as an artist and knowing that it is OK to love again. I didn't think that could be possible. But I slowly came to the understanding that I need to live in the moment and not despair of the past. Each weekend with Alan helped me understand that memories of Derrick may fade in the shadows, but they are and will always be my memories and to be cherished and treasured. The times spent with him were precious, and so were the times spent with Alan.

As I briefly looked back on the old year, I realized how far I had come in such a short time, and it was all due to the love that transpired two worlds, one visible and the other one invisible, and the knowledge that love transcends these boundaries and will never be disconnected.

CHAPTER
16

March 10 was the date of the show in Chicago. Ironically, it was close to the anniversary of Derrick's death, and I wasn't sure how I really was going to be, but there was no way out of changing the date. I simply had to be there, and be ready and focus on the day.

I had combed the malls for the perfect outfit to wear for my debut. I finally settled on a pair of print pants that sort of looked like Van Gogh's *Starry Starry Night*. It was a print legging with small swirls and suns and teamed up with a blue oversized jacket and a white knit top and chunky boots; it made me look the part of the artist. I was always a conservative dresser, but I felt that this would be the perfect outfit to express who I was, rather than a black pair of pants and an oxford shirt. Alan liked it and said it was perfect.

"My dear, you look just fabulous," Alan said, emphasizing the word *fabulous*. I twirled around and then did a pose and then a quick walk through the living room à la runway style. "Sweetheart, they are going to love you. They are going to love your paintings, and they are going to fall in love with you, like I have."

It had only been a couple of months since we seriously dated, but as he looked at me, casting an endearing look, his brown eyes sparkling, I knew he was sincere. I was feeling the same way. It wasn't that he had "discovered me" but that he believed in my work and knew I would do well.

We had four weeks to the show, and in between flying and just taking care of everyday matters, I was burning the candle at both ends and was seriously considering that if this new venture took off, that I might hang up my wings of flying. I knew I could not keep up with the hectic pace of both worlds. If I did well and worked hard enough, honing my talent and making sure my work got out there, I might make enough to live comfortably on.

It was two weeks before the show, and when I landed from a four-day trip, Alan came over to my apartment, and his face was white as a ghost.

"What is the matter?" I asked. I thought he might be ill, or there was something wrong with Lizzy that I didn't know about. "What is it? Don't keep me in suspense."

"The show in Chicago has been cancelled. The venue has been closed down."

Everything in my body just felt like a deadweight. My heart immediately felt like a hundred pounds, and I sunk down on the couch as if I just got hit in the chest by a football. I closed my eyes and started to cry.

"Don't panic!" Alan said. "I am flying to London tomorrow, and I think we might be able to squeeze you in another art showing, but it won't be for another month. There is a show of new artists on April 15. Lloyd Kirby has seen your work, and he is interested. I am going over there to persuade him to include you. It's worth a chance."

I sat there and cried thinking that it was hopeless and that all this was for nothing. I had hoped beyond hope that this would work for me, but what did it matter. Wonderful things don't happen like this to me. It all gets taken away at some point. I was beginning to feel like I lost the world. That I had wasted my time, and nothing was ever going to come to anything at all. London was a big city, and who in their right mind would take on a woman's art like mine to show. It could never happen. Maybe Chicago, maybe Minneapolis, but not London. London was an elusive dream.

Alan could see me slip away into the depths of despair. "Listen, darling. I am not going to let this fall through our fingers. I believe in you, and I am sure I can get you in with the London showing. But I have to leave tonight, and I will call you this time. I promise. I will call you with the answer, so don't fall apart on me. Think positive."

He poured me a glass of wine to steady on my nerves. I realized I would find out within forty-eight hours what my fate would be. Being a new artist was hard enough to get a showing that didn't get cancelled, or you would get accepted was another thing.

"Do you really think that they will accept me? Do you really think I could get in at such a short notice?"

Alan gave me a hug and said, "I don't know. I am going to try my hardest. Kit, your art is incredible. It has to get out there somehow, and I am going to do it if I have to sell your canvases in Hyde Park."

I felt somewhat hopeful. "Well, you know they do have an art sale on Saturdays I heard tell."

"Well, we are not going to go that route if we have to. But your art is just amazing, and it has so much life and fire. It has to be seen, and somehow we are going to do it. I am leaving for London at nine, and I will be back Sunday night. But I will call you tomorrow after I meet with Mr. Kirby. I promise."

"You better get going then," I said. I felt a bit more hopeful, but at the same time, I didn't want to get too positive, lest I be let down again. I couldn't go through it a second time.

"Keep yourself in a hopeful but grounded optimism. Keep that going, but no matter what, we are going to get your art out there."

Alan kissed me the way I had never been kissed before. His lips spoke of urgency and sincerity and yet tinged with fire and passion. *What a goodbye kiss!* I thought. I could easily live with those! He winked at me as he let himself out the door. "Keep the faith, Kit!" he said, and then he left for the airport.

I could hardly sleep at all that night. I felt that I was vicariously on his journey as I downloaded the app to watch his plane go across the Atlantic. I kept track of it until he got to the other side, and then exhaustion overtook the nervous anticipation I felt. I collapsed on the couch.

I woke up to the phone ringing. At first I was confused at the sound of the ring and was praying it wasn't crew scheduling as I would have had to say I was fatigued and unfit to fly, which I was. But it was Alan, and he sounded excited and breathless as he spoke into the phone. For a moment I didn't think I could handle any bad news, as my heart pounded out of my chest, and I was about ready to pass out. Excitedly, Alan said, "Darling, get your suitcase organized. We are flying to London in four weeks to do a show!"

"You are kidding! Really? Really?" I kept asking in disbelief. London would be the height of everything for me if I was successful, but apparently, Mr. Kirby and Alan did think the same way. I couldn't believe it. London. Of all places for a showing, that beats Chicago!

We talked about the details. He had already booked me a hotel, and I would be staying in Kensington Garden area, and the venue would not be too far from the hotel. I had flown to London so many times as a flight attendant but never with a situation like this. I then realized that I had used up my vacation for the March 10 showing, which was never going to happen, so I would be reduced to bidding the time off, and hopefully I would be able to get those days off. I wouldn't know for another two weeks, until after the bids went through, but I thought to myself, surely I would be able to get those days. I am senior enough.

The rest of the day was spent in dancing around the apartment, calling any and all of my friends that were home to be happy for me, and of course family who were twice as thrilled. I barely could eat dinner that night. Lizzy was to the moon with me when she came home and heard the story. She was spending a lot of weekends up at Eagles Mere with Colin. I was happy about that as I loved Derrick's family, and this was a way for me to still be connected to them, and Lizzy was making that possible.

CHAPTER
17

I was about to have a meltdown of the tsunami kind. The bids came out, and what I got assigned was nothing I requested. The weekend that I needed off was denied due to low reserves, and despite the fact that I could possibly trade or swap days, it wasn't working out with anyone. I might be able to take time off without pay, but it would not look good in my attendance folder, and I might have to take a dreaded missed-flight assignment. I really loved my job and the people I worked for and with. I loved flying, and I loved meeting new people and going to different places. I had made friends with people at the hotel desks, van drivers, and restaurants that I would frequent. I wasn't sure what to do as it was either I choose my job or I forget doing the show. Doing the art showing was a huge risk as there was a lot of competition, and one had to be really good and have a lot of connections to make it in the art world, and I was just a rookie. My job was secure as long as there was an airline, but I was afraid to take that risk of quitting my paying job for one that had no security and was all risk.

I knew what I had to do.

With trembling fingers, I punched Alan's number.

"Hello, Kit! Where are you? Are you home?"

"No, I am in San Francisco," I said quietly.

"So what is going on, sweetheart? How is your trip thus far?"

"It is OK. You know the usual drama that goes on. Passengers who seem to like to stuff oversize suitcases into the bins and then complain that it fit in the last plane."

I could hear Alan smile on the other end. He knew all the stories, but he still liked hearing them.

"Alan, I have something to tell you."

"What is it, sweetie?" he asked, not sensing anything was wrong on the other end.

"I am going to pull out of the show in London. I can't get the time off."

There was dead silence at the other end.

"Whaaaaaat?" he bellowed. "What? You are pulling out? Why?"

"I can't get the time off," I said quietly.

"Call in sick then!" he said in a terse tone. "You cannot pull out of this now. You have to be there. I went the second mile for you to get you in this show. I believe that you can make a success out of this! What are you saying, pull out of the show? You can't do it!"

"I am going to have to. I can't call in sick. I will have attendance issues with the airline if I do that."

"You will have issues with me, Kit! Come on now! You can't pull out of the show! You just can't."

"I have no choice," I said quietly.

"You do too! Kit! If you pull out of this at the last minute, then your career as a professional artist is over. You may not ever get another shot like this one, and sure enough, I don't think I will or could help you in the future."

"What are you saying, Alan?"

"What I am saying is, that I put a lot of time and effort into getting you into the London art show. I am saying that if you don't go through with this, I will really be upset. I mean, I am not going to leave you but, Kit, this is an opportunity of a lifetime. You cannot pull out!"

"I can't risk my career with the airlines for something that I am not so sure about." My mouth was getting dry from being anxious.

"It is a huge mistake, Kit, to pull out of the London show. Find another way. Please! I worked so hard to get you in."

"And I worked so hard to get my job as a flight attendant," I said feeling the tension rise on both ends of the phone. "If I fail as an artist, then what do I have?"

"You aren't going to fail as an artist, Kit. You have what it takes: natural talent. If I didn't think so, I wouldn't have gone the lengths that I have done to get you this far. Quit the airlines if you have to, but you have to be at that showing, or you might as well pack it all up!"

There was nothing more to be said. I didn't say yes. I was quitting the airlines, or yes, I was pulling out of the show. I had to give this some thought. I was never much the risk-taker, but I felt that I was in the fork on the road to speak, and a wrong move could prove to be fatal. Oh, where was Derrick at a time like this? He would tell me what to do. But then I realized he really had been gone. I hadn't seen him since Christmas, and even though I called out to him, there was no reappearance. I would have to figure this out on my own. And I had less than a week to make a life-changing decision.

It was hard to concentrate at work. I had to keep my distracted thoughts at bay, but at times it was hard. Was I ever glad to be cleaning up the cabin as the plane was preparing for landing. But I knew then when I landed, I would have to make the decision as to what to do. It really had to be based on what was good for me, and not everyone else. Even though I would really disappoint Alan, I had to do what was best for me and the rest of my life. Although I was hoping Alan would be in the rest of my life, if I pulled out, so might he. Could I risk that? What would Derrick tell me to do? But I had the feeling that he was long gone. His mission to get me focused and moving forward was done, and he was on the other side, enjoying whatever heaven had to offer him.

I was pondering the great mysteries of life as I was making my way through the concourse. As I walked past the food court, I noticed they were remodeling it. Funny, I hadn't paid that much attention in the last year or so about what was going on in the food court. A different style of bench was replacing the tables where I met Derrick. Everything seemed to have to change. It was inevitable. Why things couldn't stay the same was beyond me. There was a calmness and stability in sameness, but at the same time, without change or moving forward in this life, there was also stagnation. I didn't necessarily feel stagnation in my job. I still loved it as there was always something different happening with each and every flight, whether it be with passengers or flight crew or circumstances. But there were other things taking place. I missed being away from Alan. I missed my apartment, and I missed not having control of my own destiny, or as it would, my schedule. If I had control of my schedule, this would not be an issue.

I made my way out of the secured area and on my way to the train to get to the parking ramp. I looked over at the passenger pickup and fondly thought of the days that Derrick would pick me up. Him waiting for me made coming home all that more exciting. Even though Alan made my days wonderful, he was never there at the airport picking me up. Not that it mattered, but it was nice having someone wait for you after you were done with a working trip.

As I got in my car, I reflected again at all the changes. They were redoing a section of the parking garage. Everywhere I looked, there seemed to be change. And then it hit me. I knew what to do and what decision to make. I didn't need Derrick to help me find the answer. The answer was within myself.

CHAPTER
18

I went back to the airport. There was still time. I went through security and then headed toward the in-flight supervisors office. Good, she was still there.

"Karen?" I said as I knocked at the door.

"Kit! How are you? Are you coming or going?"

"Er, not sure if what you mean by that. It could possibly mean that I am coming 'but' going."

"What do you mean?" Karen asked as she turned away from her computer screen and was more focused on what I was going to say.

"I have an art showing in April, the weekend of the fifteenth. I am scheduled to work, and I can't seem to trade or swap with anyone." I was quietly hoping that she would let me take time off without pay.

"And?" Karen asked.

"I need the time off," I asked quietly.

"If you can swap it or drop it or trade it off, but just giving you the time off unless it is a family emergency or a life situation like a family wedding, I can't just give you the time off."

"Well, I can't really drop or swap, so I am going to quit. I am turning in my badge and my manual."

"What?" Karen asked shocked. "You are going to just quit?"

"Yeah, I think so. I can give in my two weeks' notice, but I am officially quitting if I can't get the time off."

"Are you sure you can't swap or drop? You are one of our best flight attendants."

"No, I tried. I really did. And I have a feeling this is a once-in-a-lifetime opportunity, and it is a huge chance I need to take."

"I understand," Karen said quietly. "We will really miss you around here."

"I know, I will miss working here too." I sighed heavily.

"If it doesn't work out, you can always come back you know," Karen said sadly. "I wish there was something we could do for you, but there really isn't."

"I know. But this is something I must do, or I may regret this for the rest of my life."

"You can turn in your badge when your last day comes. Of course, but I will be sorry to lose you, Kit. Are you sure there isn't anyone you can swap with or have someone pick your trip up?"

"I tried, but no one can help me this time round. I just have to quit, I can't afford to miss this opportunity. Thank you though for everything."

"Thank you, Kit, but please try to find someone to pick up your trips. I will hate to lose you," Karen said sadly.

When I walked out of the office, I realized I had done the right thing. I did something for myself. And I was making a change for something that I could fly to the moon with, or fail miserably, but at least, I would know that I had tried, and that was what Derrick would have wanted. He would have wanted me to take a risk, take a chance, and to move forward. That is what he was telling me all along.

And in the back of my mind I could hear him say "atta, girl."

The last two weeks of working were bitter sweet. With every landing, I realized that would be the last one and that this crazy career would be over, but a new one would possibly be taking its place. Everyone was sad to see me go. I would be missing some of the pilots and flight attendants. I had made friends with, but they promised that they would keep in touch with me, and I believed them. They all wanted me to do their portrait. Of course ... and in full uniform!

When the last day of the trip came, when I did my last compliance check and my last gathering of garbage, I felt both excited and scared. I had to make this work for me; otherwise, I wasn't sure what I would do. Having to go back to the company and going back to zero, seniority was something I didn't want to face, but there were too many people who believed in me, and I knew this would have to work.

Two weeks later, I found myself on a plane headed to London. I was going to meet Alan at Heathrow, and we were going to go to the hotel and then get ready for my showing. Alan was relieved that I wasn't pulling out of the show and admitted to some heart palpitations while waiting for me to figure out what I was going to do. When he saw me at the airport, he was overcome with joy to see me and excited to show me around London that evening. I was too tired with jet lag and stressed to go on a tour of London that I had seen so many times before that we opted out for a quiet dinner of scrambled eggs and toast with tea.

I got dressed for the show, and my heart was in my throat. I was so nervous, and my mouth was so dry that I had to walk around with a water bottle. I wasn't sure if that was kosher, but it was either that or have a dry mouth and not really be able to articulate to people who were interested in my work. I was that nervous!

My art was hung on a far wall, but I had a lot of people viewing it, and the main attraction was Derrick's portrait. It was the center of attraction, and I had some offers of up to $1,000 for just that one painting, but I could not sell it as it belonged to Mom.

The canvas paintings of birds were a hit, and I ended up selling every painting and banked over $5,000. I was *gobsmacked*. A word I used often for being totally undone, and I was. I never or would ever have made this amount of money, and all for all just a few paintings. This really surpassed what I made at the airline.

I was asked to do another show in the fall, and I decided to feature the paintings I did from the photos I took from flying over the ocean or the Rocky Mountains. The curator assured me that every painting would be sold. He told me to go back to America and go get painting.'

And I did! When I got home, I bought new paints and canvases, and I started on working on paintings for the fall show and in between took appointments to do portraits of kids, pilots of course, and pets. It was a wonderful new life, and to think that it took Derrick poking and prodding me to do something in order to move forward.

Alan and I set up a wedding date for the following year after the show. I never thought I would ever love again or want to get married. I never thought I would find my smile again, but I did. Not because I was painting and being successful at it, but I found love again as Derrick said I would. I still loved and remembered him, but with Alan, it was different but still just as sweet. Although I didn't believe Derrick at first, my story wasn't over yet; there were still many chapters yet to write in my book.

Lizzy married Colin the year after Alan and I married, and there was still that connection with Derrick's family which I appreciated. Alan didn't mind in the least bit and got on with Mom and Dad until they died, and the family home went to the eldest son, but then he got tired of the huge upkeep and then had it sold. Nothing ever stays the same. Nothing should. It should be evolving and moving forward, forever changing as life does.

CHAPTER
19

The snow is not falling as heavy as the setting sun is trying to pierce through the chalky gray sky. Nighttime will be upon us. And I enjoyed my quiet afternoon of my reverie, thinking about all the happy memories I have had in my life. I was glad for all the good times, and even the sad times proved to work itself all out. Each incident in my life proved to bring me some happiness even though some of the roads were difficult. Maybe that is what life is all about. The difficult times often get us out of our easy spot and push us to take chances that we wouldn't normally take. Derrick was trying to teach me this as he was helping me through my grief. It took him to push me to try do other things, and Alan to encourage me that sometimes the risk is worth taking. There cannot always be safety nets ready to catch us when we fall. If we do fall, then we need to learn to catch on to something so we can pause and figure out what to do next.

And nothing stays the same. Change is inevitable. If there weren't changes, then things would stagnate and become boring and deadly dull. Change shakes us up, makes us look at ourselves in a new way and to figure out what to do in the process. It helps us grow as a person, adding a new dimension to our lives so that we can become interesting to others as well as ourselves. It is a necessary part of life. Even if it is to change one's attitude which is what I so struggled with in losing Derrick. But in losing Derrick, I gained so much. Plus, the happy memories he left me.

My paintings proved to be a success. Famous people bought my paintings, as well as collectors, and I made myself a very successful living. Alan and I married not too long after that, and Lizzy married Colin the following year, thus cementing the family ties to Derrick's family, which pleased me more than anything. I loved them very much as it was upsetting to think that I might lose them because I lost Derrick. Alan loved Derrick's family and found them fun especially around the holidays as they knew how to celebrate, and there was never a dull moment.

But I am alone now. Alan died three years ago, and strangely enough, he did not haunt me like Derrick did. Just as well as it could be unnerving, but I would have loved to have heard his voice again, like I did with Derrick.

The sun is breaking through the clouds and giving the gray sky a much warmer glow. Night will be settling in soon, and it will be time for bed and not a moment too soon. My eyelids are very heavy, and I am not sure how I can hold on much longer for my nightly drink of warm milk. Nurse should be coming soon. But I am so sleepy. I just cannot hold on any longer.

"Kit!" I hear a familiar voice. I turn around, but my eyes are so heavy I cannot open them at all now.

"Kit," I hear another voice along with the first one. *What is this? Is this the new night nurse? Why are there two of them?* I still cannot open my eyes.

"Come on, Kit!" I then open my eyes. I can barely see. It's like I have a paste over my eyes. There are two men standing in front of me smiling. *Why are two men standing in front of me? Who are they?*

"Who are you?" I call out. My eyes are clear now, and I can see two figures standing before me, smiling and looking so handsome and young. Yet my surroundings are so surreal. Everything in the room is like a huge mist came over my room, and yet I see those two figures clearly as well as a small tunnel with a light at the end. But everything around the tunnel is muddled and misty. What is going on?

"Kit, it is I, Derrick. I have come to get you! It's time."

"No, I have come to get you. It's me, Alan! This fool doesn't know what he is talking about."

"Time for what? Derrick? Alan?" I asked. I am confused.

"Time to come with us," Derrick said. "Actually, I was supposed to pick you up, but this guy insisted on coming along." Derrick flashed that smile that was so familiar to Kit.

"No, I was supposed to pick her up, but you were annoying," Alan said, flashing those mischievous brown eyes at Kit.

"Actually, we started a fuss in heaven as to who was to pick you up, so it was commanded that we both do it, although I hardly see the reason why. I was your first love, other than your first ex-husband, wherever he is now!" Derrick sniggered.

"Behave!" Alan said. "I married her!"

"Well, I would have been had I not died!" Derrick said.

"Oh, stop it, boys!" I said. My eyes were clearing, and my vision was as sharp as I could ever imagine, yet my surroundings were all fuzzy and in a weird dimension. I couldn't quite figure it out.

"Then, let's go!" Derrick said as he gave me his arm, and I then linked up with Alan.

We passed the night nurse who had the tray of hot milk that she was late in giving me, very late I should wonder. We went past the reception area. Some of the residents who were dedicated night owls were still up sitting in reception, either talking to the nurses or the other residents. I stopped to say goodbye to them, but they didn't hear or see me. We walked through the door, to the outside where it was feet deep with snow. But strangely enough, I couldn't feel the cold, and then we walked toward the light that seemed to lead toward the sunset.

"This is where we are going," Derrick said. "And we have all eternity to fight over you!"

I smiled at both of them. "This is going to be interesting," I said thinking of the fuss these two were going to create but how I was going to enjoy it.

"You aren't kidding," Alan said as we moved closer and closer to the light. "Where we are going is very much beyond belief, and anything you could ever imagine. You are going to love it!"

ABOUT THE AUTHOR

Barbara Theesfeld lives in Saint Paul, Minnesota. When she is not writing, haunting bookstores, or attending the yearly Renaissance festival, she is working as a flight attendant. This is her second book, *Three O'Clock @ Hyde Park* being her first.

CPSIA information can be obtained
at www.ICGtesting.com
Printed in the USA
FFOW03n1158190218
45072812-45454FF